BENJAMIN FRANKLIN
SERIAL KILLER

Benjamin Franklin Serial Killer copyright © 2025 by Fine Cut Press
a novel by Patrick Salway
ISBN: 978-1-7353646-0-5 (paperback)
ISBN: 978-1-7353646-3-6 (ebook)
Published by Fine Cut Press First Edition, January 2026 10 9 8 7 6 5 4 3 2 1
Printed in the United States of America
Cover Design: Roderick Brydon

PUBLISHER'S NOTE This is a work of fiction. Names, characters, places, and incidents are either the product of the author's imagination or are used fictitiously.

Benjamin Franklin Serial Killer

PATRICK SALWAY

INTRODUCTION

THE CRAVEN STREET BONES

By Dr. Harrison Chapwell, Dean of the College of Forensic Sciences, Loyola University Chicago

IN 1998, A team of conservationist workers uncovered a startling discovery at the old London home of the iconic American polymath, Dr. Benjamin Franklin. Having passed through many owners since the time of Franklin's residence at 36 Craven Street, certain aspects of the home had fallen quite badly into disrepair. In recent years, the Franklin House was used as a hostel for international students—young travelers, who drank, got high, and ravaged each other in the numerous bunks of the three-story townhouse. Thanks to a receipt of funds from the Royal Society of London, of which Franklin was a member, having been awarded its highest honor, the Copley Medal, in 1736 for his famous advancements in the study of electricity rendered by the "kite and key" experiment, the "Franklin House" was finally being restored and turned into a museum. The grant of one million pounds allowed for the creation of "The Legacy Association of Dr. Benjamin Franklin," a non-profit organization responsible for restoring the home and overseeing its conversion into an operational museum. Once restored, The Franklin House would be open to the public, featuring reenactments of the supposed daily life activities of Dr. Franklin, his landlady, the Widow Mrs. Stevenson, and her daughter Mary, or "Polly" as Franklin affectionately called her. Franklin had come to regard Polly as his own daughter, having been away so long from his own children back in New World Philadelphia.

The time Franklin lived and worked in London (1751-1776) as the ambassador to the American Colonies was the most important era of his life and career. However, this period has hitherto been glazed over by the popular historical account. During Franklin's twenty-five-year stay in London, he lodged at the home of his late colleague, Dr. William Stevenson, a renowned philosopher, and fellow Freemason. Upon Stevenson's death in 1750, the home was left to his widow. One year later, Ben Franklin accepted an invitation from the Crown to live and work in London as ambassador and postmaster general to the American colonies. Unbeknownst to the statesman, fate would have him stay in England for over two decades.

The three-story red brick townhouse at 36 Craven Street features a stucco facade over the first story, which gives the illusion of stone masonry. The backyard, which was severely overgrown by the time the Legacy Association got ahold of it, stretches a quarter-acre behind the house and terminates at the "rose garden," now a messy collection of thorny, petrified sticks.

Sarah Wilson, an undergraduate student of American History at Columbia University, was studying abroad in London when she made the discovery that would forever alter the record of Ben Franklin's life—that is, if history will allow. Although it has been nearly a quarter of a century since Wilson's discovery, there is little written or known about the "Craven Street Bones," aside from the few magazine articles written on the subject in second-rate publications upon initial discovery. The story then fizzled out, quite as conspicuous as the bones themselves. The mainstream would not touch the story.

Why there is no proper investigation into this monumental finding other than the initial forensic inquiry which proved the bones were indeed from the time Franklin lodged at the house, is still a mystery. It seems as if the writers of history are reluctant to indulge the macabre possibilities lying dormant within the Craven Street Bones. Judging by the condition in which they were found, one can be certain they have a ghastly story to tell to any journalist brave enough to investigate. Nearly all of the skulls shared a signature hole in the center of the cerebellum, presumably from a trepanning device—a crude, hand-cranked drill.

However, today's media is not interested in marring the legacy of America's benevolent grandfather, who for some reason, was never president, yet whose face adorns the highest note of American currency and whose stamp marks every important passage in early American history. It is as if Franklin's influence pulled the strings behind every major advancement in American life during the 1700s, including liberation from the Crown of England in 1776, the year he was booted out of that country in disgrace for inciting a series of Colonial riots that eventually lead to the Revolutionary War by deliberately leaking incendiary letters between the British Parliamentary official Andrew Oliver and then Massecuests governor, Thomas Hutchinson. Their correspondence detailed a proposition by the Crown to tax the American Colonists to high heaven in order to subvert their mounting power and prevent them from ever gaining independence. Ben Franklin: Revolutionary.

By the time Sarah Wilson's shovel hit an iron trap door in the ground beside the stone flower bed of dead rose bushes at 36 Craven Street, Benjamin Franklin was simply a jolly historical figure who tied a key to a kite and flew it in a lightning storm. The picture of morality, frugality, and conviviality. To the more educated Franklin fans, he was the inventor of the first convection oven, "The Franklin Stove," along with oddities like the Glass Armonica, a musical instrument comprised of a series of glass bowls stacked horizontally and played by dragging wet fingers along the turning crystal rims which produced ethereal tones said to drive the listener to suicidal depression or insanity. Ben Franklin: writer and printer of the colonies' most-read publication, *Poor Richard's Almanac*. Ben Franklin: Freemason and founder of the first Colonial secret society, the Junto, and then later, the American Philosophical Society. Now, thanks to the discovery of the Craven Street Bones made by Sarah Wilson and her shovel, Ben Franklin: Serial Killer.

Wilson summoned a few of her colleagues to assist in lifting the heavy trap door, which was encrusted to the ground, now being opened for the first time in over two hundred years. With lit flashlights illuminating a network of thick cobwebs going all the way down a dilapidated wooden staircase into a dark abyss, the conservationist workers descended the rickety wooden steps, swatting at cobwebs along the way. Upon reaching the earthen ground floor of this Georgian London tomb, Wilson's flashlight rested on a square stone box in the basement corner, rising about a foot high and four feet long. With some effort, the three conservationists successfully removed the stone slab to reveal a pile of a dozen or more human skeletons heaped one on top of the other inside of the stone box. Six of the fifteen complete skeletons were those of children (the forensic investigation carbon dated the bones to the exact time Franklin lodged at the home, as aforementioned).

The few who have chosen to write about the Craven Street Bones have conveniently explained them away as the work of Dr. William Hewson, the young husband of Polly Stevenson and resident anatomist at 36 Craven Street. Although Hewson certainly had plenty to do with the bones in the basement, there is no world in which the insatiably curious Dr. Benjamin Franklin did not know about them.

In fact, it was Franklin who was the reason they were there, having been merely assisted by Dr. William Hewson, who is now regarded as the "Father of Hematology," for his early advancements in the study of the blood. It is important to discern why, two hundred years later, no writer on the subject has been willing to engage the awful truth behind the Craven Street Bones, and the serial killer who perpetrated these crimes—Ben Franklin.

As Dean of the College of Forensic Sciences at Loyola University Chicago, I, Dr. Harrison Chapwell, am obliged to risk my life and reputation to give the first meaningful account of and explanation for the existence of the Craven Street Bones. Everything you are about to read here is historical fact, exhumed from the dark annals of history, transcribed from original copies of letters written between the principal players, collected over years spent in libraries, catacombs, and masonic lodges of England, France, and the United States. I have compiled a mountain of evidence into novelistic prose, for the sake of an easy, enjoyable read, with the hope of reaching as many people as possible. The facts contained herein are threads that could unravel the tapestry of Western History as we know it, or rather, as it has been manufactured and sold to us. If I should die suddenly of a heart attack, or in an automobile accident, or be found hanging in my room, know that I was purposely killed for writing what you are now about to read.

CHAPTER 1

WILLIAM HEWSON'S DEFINING MOMENT

Hexam, Northumberland, England, 1750.

A WOODEN COFFIN small enough for a child with a cross carved into the top lay inside of a freshly dug grave. A handful of dirt splattered across the surface with a *thud*, then another, and another. Above, the mourners surrounded the hole in the earth, listening to an Anglican Vicar recite verse from a small, tattered bible. The Vicar, pale from years of living amongst monks behind damp and stony walls in the hinterlands of England's grey north, wore a long dark green velvet robe and matching floppy hat with a solemn black sash of sanctity draped over his slight, concave chest.

"All go to the same place," he droned.

A stoic woman wearing a long black mourning dress and black velvet hooded cape wiped the dirt from her hands and nodded to a little boy with far-away eyes standing beside her. The boy was dressed in navy blue knickers and a frock with a white ruffled shirt underneath, his hair parted to the side.

"Go ahead, William," his mother said.

The boy picked up a handful of moist dirt and studied it for a moment. An earthworm slithered out of the dirt in his open palm. The boy plucked the worm and placed it in his side coat pocket before his mother noticed. Elders seldom know what motivates the whims of a child, and William Hewson, aged five, resents prying questions from condescending adults, including his own mother. Since earliest memory, William's best friend and confidant was his twin sister, Diana, presently lying inside of the wooden coffin at the bottom of the hole. Though a stark lesson in death lay right before his eyes, he was all cried out days ago when she went away for good. No physician could help her ailment of the blood, though they certainly tried to bleed the bad blood out. William decided then and there that once he was old enough, he would do whatever it took to succeed where those physicians failed. He was determined to understand the blood—how it worked, how it moved throughout the body, and how to fix it when it went bad. Now, he couldn't wait to be through with this morbid business of burying the dead to get home to his beloved pet owl, Primrose, to see how quickly she would devour the tasty earthworm squirming in his side coat pocket.

"Go on William," his mother urged. She nudged him from his musings and he tossed the dirt into the open grave while the tiresome Vicar droned on.

"And to dust, all shall return," the Vicar said.

William's mother had also cried the last of her tears when her daughter died. The year prior she had lost Dr. William Hewson Sr., her husband and the father of her children, to consumption. All northern England winters were bad, but last year was particularly severe. One day, he woke up coughing blood and was dead within a week, leaving his wife with two children to feed on his quickly drying physician's pension. She was unable to save her own daughter's life when her blood went bad, and though she took the responsibility upon herself, her resolve was stronger than her grief. She had to see this through, for the sake of her son and sole companion, William. As soon as he was old enough, he would follow in his father's footsteps as a great physician and surgeon. Maybe he would care for her if she were lucky enough to live to the ripe old age of fifty. At thirty-three, she was already well beyond middle-aged, motherhood having been thrust upon her unexpectedly, double-fold, well past her prime. In the town of Hexham, Northumberland, most girls conceived and bore their first children by the time they were fifteen—no doubt, she was a late bloomer.

CHAPTER 2

THE NEWCASTLE INFIRMARY

MUSING ON THE past was all fine and good when there was nothing to be done, but at the moment, Hewson had a big task before him that lay behind the imposing walls of the Newcastle Infirmary. He had to convince his father's old colleague, Dr. Richard Lambert, that he was man enough to shoulder the responsibilities of a medical intern. At ten years old, Hewson exhibited more mature qualities than his contemporaries, having been thrust further out into adulthood by the early tragedy of losing his father, then twin sister, and now, an ailing, aged mother to care for. She was nearing forty years old, and the winters were taking a deeper toll on her health. Thankfully, it was now springtime and Hewson was confident she would make it at least until next winter without getting sick, but time was not on his side. He shook himself from his daydream of the past—that defining moment when he buried his twin sister and resolved to learn the study of the blood in order to help others who were similarly afflicted. Then summoning his courage, Hewson traipsed up the verdant hill toward the towering Newcastle Infirmary, ready to confront the stony Dr. Lambert, whom he had met only once when he was almost too young to remember.

Inside the vast infirmary, probably the largest building the country-bred Hewson had ever stepped inside of, a nurse caught sight of the boy and, though she gave him a sideways glance when he asked to be directed to the Office of Dr. Richard Lambert, the director of the facility, she did so, without further hesitation. Hewson possessed the gift of appearing certain of himself, even when he had no idea what he was doing, which was most of the time. When he needed it, he seemed to fall into the right situations at the right time, and he knew how to harness his powers of persuasion. This certainly was the time to fan the flames of his persuasive qualities—he was entering the wooden office of Dr. Richard Lambert.

Lambert, sitting behind his large desk writing a treatise on blood-letting, deposited his quill in the inkwell after questioning the nurse as to why she had brought him a boy. William decided to speak for himself.

"Dr. Lambert, my name is William Hewson, son of your late colleague, Dr. William Hewson of Hexham, Northumberland."

Lambert, cautious though put in good humor at the memory of his late colleague, stood and beckoned the boy inside. He looked as tall and thin as a dead tree in his long black frock, white frilly shirt collar, and white hair curled just above his ears in two perfect tubes.

"William, come in, my boy. I believe the last time I saw you I had freshly delivered you from your mother's womb. Please, sit down. To what do I owe this surprising visit?"

"I am now of age where I am ready to begin my training as a physician."

Lambert let loose a chuckle.

"I appreciate your earnest desire, but what may I ask is the rush? You can't be more than ten years old."

"Some years ago my twin sister died from bad blood. Now, my

mother is aged and ailing. The winters are growing harder on her cough and my father's small pension is nearly all dried up. When my sister passed, I made it my duty to learn the blood as soon as I was old enough. Now, we are out of money and my mother is in no condition to make it through another winter like the last one. Please teach me all you know. I promise I will make an excellent understudy."

"I must warn you, I am not an easy master," the elder replied. "What makes you think you can handle this gruesome work at your tender age?"

William felt his own blood rising. He hated being talked down to as if he were a child. The young Hewson was all too aware of the uglier side of life–the loss he had endured thus far had entitled him to be treated as an adult among adults. Still, he held his tongue. His mother needed him to get this job and besides, an oath is an oath.

"I will go to any lengths in order to understand the blood."

This response perplexed the old doctor.

"Understand the blood?"

"Yes. We all have it and still, we know so little about it."

Dr. Lambert laughed. "Who told you that, my boy?" he said.

"No one told me that. My twin sister died when we were small children. She had bad blood, and no physician could help her. I feel it is my duty to succeed where those men failed. My blood is good."

It was at this moment that time seemed to slow and Hewson noticed his surroundings. He was finally in a real infirmary, talking to the headmaster about a job. A full-sized human skeleton propped up on a pole stood behind the desk where Dr. Lambert sat. A large gold ring featuring an eye inside of a triangle adorned one of the master's fingers.

"Rather odd," William thought, but he decided to forgo inquiry. Lambert seemed about ready to offer him a job and he thought it best to stay on topic.

Hewson's reply about his sister's death seemed to sober Lambert. Finally, he was beginning to see the boy as a viable prospect.

"I see. Well, you are in luck. No shortage of blood here, my boy."

Lambert stood again, his imposing figure towering over the boy as tall as the green velvet curtains hanging behind the skeleton in an otherwise stark room. Lambert's golden ring with an eye inside of a triangle looked to Hewson like it was big enough to weigh the old master's arm to the floor.

"Come, follow me," Lambert said.

Hewson followed the old doctor down a corridor to a large open room where beds lined the walls, each containing a sick patient. A woman in a canvas dress and bonnet tended to an iron cauldron situated above an open flame at the front of the room. She almost flinched upon seeing Lambert.

"Hello, Doctor!" she burst.

Lambert kept moving, saying nothing. He seemed to have this effect on all of the nurses. It was obvious he was the man in charge. It felt good to be led by a powerful, knowledgeable man of high influence.

"I am going to see to it that you learn this craft entirely," he said to the boy.

Upon closer inspection of the sick patients, Hewson could see they were lower class. Men and women with dirty faces, ratty hair, and missing teeth. The men had three-day beards or worse. Lambert and his new understudy stopped at the foot of one of the beds. Another meek nurse was tending to a female patient, using a rag and bowl of water to wipe puss from the lesions on her dirty, fever-tortured face. The patient writhed violently, eyeballs rolling back in her head, tongue searching around the outside of her mouth as if possessed by a demon.

"This woman is suffering from The Pox. A real Covent Garden nun, I suspect," Lambert said, filling a brass syringe with liquid mercury from a glass apothecary vial.

"Quicksilver. A potent cathartic."

Lambert injected the shot into the patient's right shoulder, causing a thick stream of saliva to pour out of her mouth and down her neck, her tongue still wildly searching the outside of her mouth. Then, the old doctor produced a handheld brass instrument from his breast pocket.

"This is a fleam," he said.

Lambert opened the instrument and showed it to Hewson. The fleam contained several blades—each one was a different size and they resembled small hatchets. The nurse tied a cloth tourniquet around the patient's upper right arm. Then, she extended the arm over an empty wooden bowl sitting on the bedside table and held it in place.

"We will use the largest blade," Lambert said. "She has big veins."

Lambert clicked the smaller blades back inside of the fleam so that only the largest blade remained open. Hewson watched closely as Lambert placed the blade to the patient's bulging forearm vein. Then, picking up a small wooden bat from the bedside, he whacked the back of the blade causing a knick on the vein that produced a heavy blood flow into the bowl.

"Just like tapping a keg. Give it a try." Lambert said, holding the instrument out to Hewson.

Hewson took the instrument from Lambert's hands, then placed the blade to the vein about half an inch from the bleeding wound.

"That's it. Now give it a good whack. Don't worry, she doesn't know where she is," the old doctor advised.

Hewson summoned up his nerve and whacked the end of the fleam, sending a fresh stream of dark blood into the bowl.

"You have a light hand," Lambert said.

Hewson wasn't sure if having a light hand was a bad thing, but the master looked pleased.

"The chief requirement of a fine surgeon."

CHAPTER 3

HEWSON GOES TO EDINBURGH

THE YEARS PASSED for young William Hewson, working under the tutelage of Dr. Lambert at the Newcastle Infirmary, poking holes in the arms of the infirmed and letting their blood. The old doctor paid his young assistant a decent salary for his menial labor. Hewson earned enough to cover his basic needs and those of his aging mother, but alas, she was not long for this world. She passed in an especially brutal winter, three years later. Her death was hard on Hewson, as were the losses of all those close to him, but by then he was a young man of thirteen and well accustomed to death and dying. Besides, his work at the infirmary kept him busy. Dr. Lambert had given him a research position to help further his study of the blood and Hewson took to it in a rabid fashion, partly to outrun the grief nipping at his back, though even he was unaware of his motivation. All he wanted to do was throw himself deeper into his work and this he did.

Dr. Lambert equipped Hewson with a microscope and slides and allowed him to take samples from patients as needed. Eventually, through a research essay entitled, "The Shape Of Red Blood Cells," Hewson won a scholarship to study in Edinburgh, Scotland where he studied under the renowned physician Dr. William Hunter, earning his doctorate in the study of the blood in the process.

Having been back at the Newcastle Infirmary for several years working as an accredited physician, Dr. Hewson had his own understudy whom he taught to let blood and administer ointments and tinctures when they were available. The boy's name was Magnus Falconer and he started at the infirmary at around the same age William did, though not even Magnus himself knew how old he was. Magnus was an orphan, born to a drunken mother on the streets of London's Gin Lane. One day, he hopped on the back of a rag cart bound for the countryside and eventually made it all the way up north to Newcastle Upon Tyne—as far from Gin Lane as the rag cart would take him. Magnus had a strong desire to help others and was very obedient. He had no problem focusing all of his attention directly on the task at hand, a quality most rare in boys his age. Like Hewson, he possessed a wisdom beyond his years, earned from a life heavy with grief and hardship from the beginning.

Magnus had found the good life working at the infirmary. He took to any task with a quiet zest so attractive, it didn't take much to convince Dr. Lambert that Magnus Falconer would be a sufficient replacement for Hewson while he was away at his studies in Edinburgh.

When Hewson returned, he found a highly capable young man in his stead. Magnus had achieved a certain mastery over the tasks for which Hewson was responsible before his three-year diversion to Scotland. The roles among men were quickly changing for the better at the Newcastle Infirmary, for Dr. Lambert was now beyond a ripe old age and mostly spent his days writing correspondence to colleagues, friends, and family from his upstairs office, leaving the carrying out of day-to-day operations to Hewson and his understudy, Magnus. Hewson was now a real doctor, having studied under the finest anatomist in the British Isles, Dr. William Hunter, who graduated him at the top of his class. Now, he was the chief and sole surgeon at the Newcastle Infirmary, pulling tumors from the bodies of the lowest classes, sewing them back up, and seeing them through a hopeful recovery, for healthful recoveries were often rare. Hewson cared for his sick patients as a stable master might attend to one of his sick horses—with much discretion but also, a degree of separation. One cannot get too close, lest one be pulled under the tide of cumulative loss.

Although he was now the chief surgeon at the Infirmary, having Magnus at his disposal allowed Hewson more time to devote to his research, with which he became increasingly engaged, having gone back to his initial entry to the study of anatomy he found in his youth—working with animal subjects. While studying in Scotland under Dr. William Hunter, Hewson was afforded ample opportunities to cut open and examine the insides of real human cadavers, which was indeed rare, not only for the nature of the act but because studying the science of anatomy on human corpses had been outlawed in Europe for hundreds of years. In fact, the practice was punishable by death. The Church deemed this an unholy act of desecration of the severest degree, and therefore, devout naturalists had to acquire their subjects through criminal means, either by purchasing a body that was hanged at the gallows from the hangmen's slaves or from the resurrectionist men—a raucous class of pirates who exhumed corpses from freshly dug graves, for a pretty penny, of course. Some went so far as to justify murder for the practice of studying the body while it was closest to its living state as possible. The direst occultists even practiced a kind of torture on the living, in order to see the inner workings of the body in action. Such rogues developed a reputation rather quickly and Dr. William Hunter was certainly not one of them. His career in academia spoke for itself— he had long-developed connections with the best bodysnatchers not only in the British Isles but in Spain and Portugal, as well. If there was anyone who could safely secure a quality body for the study of anatomy, it was Dr. William Hunter. Hewson felt an immediate kinship with the renowned surgeon, who in turn, took a fair liking to the young intern. The two developed a fine working relationship, Master and Student, and Dr. Hunter often said the day would come when he would summon Hewson to assist in lectures at the Anatomical Society he was busy forming. Dr. Hunter had secured a building in London's Gin Lane, hidden amongst the derelicts and houses of ill repute, where Albion's best anatomists could come together to do their work without hindrance of any kind from the University, the State, or the Church.

Such a call did indeed come one particularly quiet morning when Hewson was at work in his humble laboratory in the cellar at the Newcastle Infirmary, studying a live turtle trapped in a vice. Hewson's soul throbbed with a deep connection to all living beings. Although he had been using reptiles as his anatomical subjects since boyhood, it was part of his practice to beg the forgiveness of his cold-blooded friends before making the first incision. His studies were for the greater good of man. If Hewson was less sure of his ability to be uniquely useful in unlocking the secret mysteries of nature that lie dormant within living creatures, waiting for discovery, his conscience might get the better of him, he thought. As Hewson pet the turtle's head, he spoke to it in soothing tones.

"Thank you for your sacrifice, Old Schroder. Know that your legacy will live on through the countless lives our research will go on to save."

With that, Hewson filled a brass syringe with quicksilver from one of the many glass apothecary vials on his shelf.

"Please forgive me, old friend."

It was at this moment the feeble Dr. Lambert entered holding a letter.

"William, my boy. It seems as if you've received correspondence from your old schoolmaster."

The wisdom glistening in the old man's eyes suggested he already knew the contents of the unopened letter and was prepared for the outcome, whatever it may be. The fates were turning in their spheres and soon Dr. Lambert would be among them. He was more than ready to let this world and everything in it go. His big ring with "The Eye Of Providence" within a triangle shone in the candlelight as he handed the letter to Hewson, who set down his brass syringe beside the writhing turtle, spared for the moment.

CHAPTER 4

A LONDON WALK WITH ERASMUS DARWIN AND DR. BENJAMIN FRANKLIN

ON A GREY-BLACK Georgian London morning, a thick layer of toxic smoke forever lingers in the air. Black smoke billows out of chimneys from every visible structure, often several chimneys to one building, like mushrooms sprouted from cow patties in an endless field of rock, brick, and mortar. The cobblestone streets are crowded with dirty peasants, gossiping politicians, noblemen in high wigs, and clergy in their velvet. There is a light sprinkling of skeletal tramps guzzling from half-empty bottles of fiery gin. Rich or poor, one in five people on the street suffer from incurable syphilis lesions oozing on their bodies. One infected noble has attempted to cover the open lesions on his face with an extra thick layer of powdery white make-up, and to no avail—he looks the most ghastly of all. A small group of macaroni youth enjoys a dull, airy laugh in unison, completely unenthused. Their style of dress is utterly flamboyant; leopard fur knickers, towering white wigs stacked four feet high above their heads, burgundy velvet smocks, and gigantic polka dot bow ties, their faces painted up like psychedelic geishas with pasty white make-up and round red rosy cheeks.

In this milieu, Dr. Benjamin Franklin and his friend and trusted colleague, Erasmus Darwin, walk the cobblestone streets with their skinny canes.

"Any luck finding a new candidate?" asks Darwin, his plump round face probing and inquisitive.

"I have a prospect in mind," says Dr. Benjamin Franklin in his easy-going way.

"Do tell."

"A certain William Hewson has been the understudy of our dear friend Sir Richard Lambert at the Newcastle Infirmary for the better part of a decade. I have heard through the grapevine that Dr. William Hunter..."

"Oh, that pompous bastard." Darwin interrupts.

"...is hot to poach the boy for his Anatomical Society. I intend to poach him from the poacher. Keep him in the family."

"I've never had cause to doubt you, brother Franklin. We meet upon the level..."

"And part upon the square."

The men shake hands, Darwin's hand covering Franklin's in the secret "Lion's Paw" handshake—the real grip of a master mason.

CHAPTER 5

HEWSON GOES TO LONDON

AFTER SEVERAL DAYS' travel by coach from Newcastle Upon Tyne, Hewson arrived at the London home of Dr. William Hunter on a late and foggy night. Three brass knocker raps on a large wooden door put him face-to-face with a towering African slave dressed in a long black frock over a crimson coat and white silk knickers. The slave greeted Hewson with a nod and ushered him inside the grand home with a gentle motion of the oil lamp he held in his hand. Although the young doctor was certainly well educated, he had lived his entire life in the Albion north, where slavery was not nearly as fashionable as it was in the fast moving city of London. Hewson heard rumors of wealthy families who owned slaves in Edinburgh, and he was well aware of the booming trade in the New World and the cruelty with which those unfortunate souls were treated, but this was the first time he had met an African in real life. In fact, this was the first time Hewson had met a person who was not of direct Anglo-Saxon descent, and he was humbly fascinated. The slave said nothing, leading the awe-struck surgeon down a candlelit hallway, replete with the trimmings of London's well-to-do. Heavy velvet, candelabras, strange Far-East tapestries, and silver finery all around.

Dr. Hunter, dressed in forest green, floor-length velvet frock, and cap, was at work assembling a mostly complete human skeleton propped up on a pole. Long accustomed to the highly illegal exchange of money for bodies that happened under the cover of darkness, Hunter always worked at night. The elder anatomist followed the health habits of his idol, Leonardo DaVinci, taking in sleep only fifteen minutes at a time, every two hours. In this way, he was highly prolific in his work, and pasty pale-white, with large dark bags that hung deep beneath his wide, darting eyes. Hunter's laboratory was littered with complete human skeletons propped up on poles, large egg-shaped oriental urns sitting on pedestals, glass apothecary vials of clear and amber liquids neatly organized by size on shelves lining the walls, floor to high ceiling. In front of the shelves sat a white linen-covered table that displayed an array of strange tools: knives, scalpels, pliers, and small hand-cranked drills, with larger pliers and drills hanging on the wall behind.

A knock on the door startled Dr. Hunter, who was concentrating on attaching vertebrae to the thoracic spine, nearly prompting the old sleep-deprived surgeon to drop a bone.

"You may enter," Hunter said in formal tones, a surplus of baggy skin hanging under his weak chin.

In walked Hunter's slave like a praying mantis, followed by his best student from the Edinburgh days.

"Hello, Dr. Hunter."

"Ah, if it isn't William Hewson, the promising young surgeon. Thank you for accepting my invitation and traveling all the way from Newcastle Upon Tyne."

Hunter set the vertebrae on a silver dish to greet his understudy with a proper handshake.

Hewson blushed and fiddled with his tricorn hat in hand. Five years had passed since he had seen his old mentor, during which time he had single-handedly run all of the surgeries at the Newcastle Infirmary. He was a doctor, a surgeon with a good reputation, thanks to the man standing before him, who took a keen interest in developing his skills while they were in Edinburgh. Hewson's heart swelled with gratitude for his old schoolmaster. It was good to receive this compliment, though he was quite unsure of what to do with it.

"Indeed, it was a long journey, but a pleasurable one. Your coachman is highly skilled and the countryside offered many fine sights," he said.

"Well, it is a pleasure to have you here in London, my boy. I hope Dr. Lambert was not too ill-disposed in lending out his lead surgeon for a time in order to help advance an old naturalists' cause," Hunter said.

"He was quite gracious about it, sir. My understudy, Magnus, has taken to the practice of surgery with a keen eye and a light hand. I am sure he will have no trouble at all keeping things in order," Hewson replied.

Hunter smiled large, his eyes wide and full of pleasure at having not put Dr. Lambert in a difficult position.

"That is welcome news, indeed. I would hate to compromise Dr. Lambert's operation in the slightest, but I feel our cause is worthy. I read your recent report on the lymphatic system, and I must say, I was impressed. The findings from your curious experiments are quite astonishing..."

This even more deeply reddened the blushing Hewson.

"...but reptiles can only take you so far," Dr. Hunter warned. "I want to employ you full-time as the lead surgeon during my lectures at the Anatomical Society. In turn, I shall offer a generous wage, along with room and board. You will have full access to my laboratory where you may continue your research between lectures."

The offer floored Hewson. Although he half-expected this to be the reason for his visit, hearing the words re-arranged his future in the most favorable light, right before his mind's eye. Here was an opportunity to be fully devoted to the study of the blood—to gain a true understanding in a lab where real breakthroughs were possible. He accepted without hesitation.

"I would be honored, sir."

"Good," Hunter said. "I've ordered us a cadaver."

CHAPTER 6

THE RESURRECTIONIST MEN

THAT EVENING, THE Resurrectionist Men were hard at work digging up a fresh grave with picks and shovels and passing around a bottle of rotgut gin.

"Easy digging tonight, boys. I love a late funeral," said the fat one, taking his turn on the bottle with his pick slung over one shoulder.

"Easy for you to say, scrubby puff guts," said one of two emaciated fellows doing the hard digging inside of the grave. "We're doing the work."

"Shut your ass, Duke Of Limbs. A pull on this might bolster your spirits."

The fat one passed the bottle down into the grave. The skinny toothless one took a long pull, his concave chest heaving against the firewater. He managed to keep it down through sheer force of will and passed it along to his partner. The fat one laughed.

"You poor poppet. You look like death's head upon a mopstick!"

After some more digging, one of their shovels hit the wooden top of the coffin.

"That'll do plenty, gollumpus. Get down here with that pick and help us pry the top off this box," the skinny one said.

"Pry it off yourselves, Jackanapes," the fat one barfed, taking another pull on the gin.

Using their shovels for leverage, the skinny ones pried off the coffin top without any trouble. One of their shovels got a good hold under the lid and with a single pry, broke the cheap wood in half. They pulled it off, revealing the body of a fresh corpse. The fat one watched from above, finishing a long, powerful swill from the bottle.

"He'll fetch a pretty penny," he said.

The resurrectionists inside the grave each grabbed an arm and yanked the corpse upright.

"He ain't even stiff yet," one of them said.

The fat one crouched down, grabbing ahold of the body wherever he could, and as the others pushed from below, dragged the corpse from the grave. Then they slung the body onto a wooden cart and with swinging lanterns and clinking tools, rolled recklessly away, leaving a mess behind.

Hunter and Hewson stood in the shadows on the bank of the misty River Thames, awaiting their morbid cargo. A sudden whistle from the water signaled their arrival as the bodysnatchers rowed out of the fog and docked alongside the anatomists. The fat one jumped out and tied the boat as the surgeons approached and peered inside to find their body covered in a dirty woolen blanket. One of the gaunt bodysnatchers wearing a ratty tricorn hat pulled the blanket aside, showing them the goods with a toothless grin. The anatomists were pleased by the sight of a fresh specimen with no signs of decay. The gaunt ones rewrapped the body and disembarked the vessel, one holding the arms and the other, the feet, and after a near spill into the murky river Thames, made it onto the bricks and heaved the dead weight onto Hunter's wooden cart, sending up a tuft of hay. Dr. Hunter produced a satchel of coins and handed it to one of the gaunt men, who selected a shilling and with some of the few teeth left in his head, bit down on it hard to test its authenticity. The mangy hyena gave a maniacal toothless laugh as they disappeared into the early morning fog.

Hewson grabbed ahold of the cart and followed Dr. Hunter, pushing their cargo through the cobblestone streets of early morning London toward Gin Lane. A few drunks lay sprinkled on the streets passed out in gutters, but when the pair arrived at Gin Lane the streets were alive with the living dead drunk on gin. Hewson caught sight of one swaying fat lady sitting atop a wooden staircase breastfeeding an infant while drinking from a bottle of rotgut. She dropped her baby off of the stairs with a delayed reaction and took another swill from the bottle. The country-bred Hewson thought the drunks in the street looked like the skeletons in Hunter's laboratory and he watched in horror as they vomited, brawled, and shouted their pain into the black sky. Many of them had oozing syphilis lesions on their faces and arms and stumbled over the stones like hunchbacks. He even saw a few faces missing noses. Deformed, toothless faces, drooping and bloodshot, rotting like pumpkins. The creaking wheel of a rusty iron weathercock spinning around atop the empty brokerage where Hewson now stood added a musical quality to the cacophony of horrid voices, breaking glass and human flesh beating stone. He lost himself for an eternity, standing in the home of forgotten souls, taking in the song of death. Around and around the iron cock spun with the wind and around again with another gust. Men lay sprawled before him in the streets, in the gutters, crawling on their bellies like slugs through muck and slime. Men and women—human beings—fighting with dogs for the last scrap of meat on a bone. Human beings struggling for survival while calling on the Angel of Death. Hewson had cared for patients in Dr. Lambert's infirmary who would bite through a cork while losing a limb, refusing gin or even laudanum, because they had survived the purgatory through which these souls crawled. The people of Gin Lane were certainly human, and if given a chance, might free themselves from this web–but they were hypnotized by their captor. They were men reduced to flies struggling through sticky white scum toward spider jaws. A fresh shot of venom, then oblivion.

The buildings on Gin Lane were a mess of wooden beams thrown every which way. Two-hundred year old butcher shops, brokerage firms, and clocktowers that resembled piles of sticks gathered up and hastily assembled into structures. Some menacing child had built this play town, only to populate it with crippled mice with which to feed its hungry pet viper.

"Have you seen such degradation?" Dr. Hunter asked as a thin smile stretched across his face. Hewson, who was still stunned before this painting of Dante, replied he had not.

"'Tis' a shame we have been relegated to the depths of hell by the Church and the State, to conduct our studies in secret, like moles in their tunnels," Hewson said.

Hunter placed his hand on Hewson's shoulder.

"But the knowledge we find here will lift up mankind," he said.

They continued on, pushing their corpse over the stones, weaving between bodies not yet dead. Hewson caught sight of a wooden structure missing most of its boards. Inside, the shadow of a body swayed to and fro, tied to the rafters.

CHAPTER 7

Dr. Hunter's Great Windmill Street Anatomical Theatre

THE PAIR TURNED down Great Windmill Street and arrived at a large stone building. Dr. Hunter stuck a key in the tall door and opened it for Hewson, who wheeled the body inside of the massive, dark chamber.

"Welcome to the Great Pyramid," Dr. Hunter said as he lit several oil lamps.

The light brought the full splendor of his Anatomical Theatre closer within view, though it was still very dark. Hewson and Dr. Hunter flopped the body from the cart to a round tabletop situated at the center of the room. Surrounding the operating table was a viewing deck hovering several feet above, where the Society Fellows would soon be watching the procedure commence.

Hewson was nervous at having an audience while performing surgery but more so, excited to be part of a research community that would bring him closer to his goal of understanding the inner workings of the human body. This was simply the next step. He told himself that fear was a sign he was shedding his old skin and advancing into new and fruitful territory.

Daylight flooded in through high windows, illuminating the full glory of Dr. Hunter's Anatomical Theatre. Hewson had never seen a thing so grand. Two full skeletons propped up in archway inlets etched into the high walls flanked a tall throne, capped with the pinecone insignia of the Anatomical Society. Pinecones were a theme—some of the pillars supporting the rail on the viewing platform surrounding the operating area were adorned with them.

Surgeons and anatomists flooded in from afar and soon enough, the lecture was in motion. Dr. Hunter, seated at his pinecone-capped throne, addressed the Society Fellows, dressed in flowing velvet robes, powdered wigs, and stiff square or floppy round academic hats, who packed the viewing platform, their quills poised at the ready above their paper journals.

"Welcome, travelers and countrymen," Dr. Hunter began.

"Some of you have labored a several days journey from Italy, France, and Spain to be with us this morning. The Society applauds your commitment to carrying this knowledge into your own countries, that we may serve our people well, though the Church and the State would not have it."

Hewson stood over the corpse in the pit between two other surgeons—a chubby man wearing a square cap with a dumb expression stamped permanently on his face, and a thin limp man who resembled a salamander at the corpses' feet. Some of the Society Fellows had brought their slaves to assist in the operation. One of them who was busy building a fire under a massive iron cauldron had got the flames going and was stirring the water with a large wooden stick, to boil the empty corpse down to bone after the operation so that Hunter could build another skeleton. The dumb-looking fat man screwed a threaded brass hook into the top of the cadaver's head and hung it around a rope connected to a pulley system hanging from the high ceiling. He pulled the other end of the rope taut, which hoisted the cadaver's head and torso up off the table, giving the men easy access to the body. Dr. Hunter proceeded, in Latin. This slapped Hewson back into reality, for he was now very tired, having been up the whole night. It had been five years since his time studying under Dr. Hunter in Edinburgh and his Latin was rusty. The gaze of the expectant Society Fellows sobered him up and his heart raced once Hunter had concluded the formal introductions and began addressing the surgeons. From the throne and using a long pointer stick, Dr. Hunter outlined an area on the torso, directing them in Latin.

"Make your incision from navel to nape and disembowel the body," Hunter commanded.

Hewson poked his scalpel into the navel sending up a dark pool of burgundy blood that became quite messy when, with some effort, he sawed his way through the rubbery flesh to the throat.

"Bleed the feet," the Master of ceremonies said.

The salamander surgeon sliced the bottom of both feet wide open with his scalpel, draining the blood from the body into a large wooden bucket on the floor.

Next, Hunter addressed the chubby dumb-faced surgeon at the head of the corpse.

"The pinecone-shaped organ behind the forehead is the pineal gland, the organ which Descartes believed to house the human soul. The art of trepanning is required, for it lies inside the brain, protected by the skull..."

Hunter tapped the corpse's forehead with his pointing stick, right between the eyes. The dumb-faced surgeon chewed on his tongue while fiercely drilling into the scalp, sending up ringlets of skin like potato peels. The sight disturbed Hewson, not so much for the gore of it all—he was used to that—but for the fact that the man chewed on his tongue like a dumb ape. Hewson was busy passing the guts to one of the slaves who piled them into a wooden bucket on the floor when a skinny dog ran up to the bucket and chewed a stray piece of the intestine. The slave shooed the mangy mut away. Dr. Hunter described the innards of the body in Latin as the Society Fellows scribbled furiously in their journals. The dumb-faced surgeon reached into the forehead of the corpse with his big gummy forefinger and thumb. After squishing around a bit, the surgeon successfully extracted the tiny pinecone-shaped pineal gland. He held it up to the light, considering it dumbly like an ape entranced by a shiny object. The din of the rabble increased amongst the Society Fellows as they scribbled away with feathery quills.

Soon, the lecture concluded and the Society Fellows filed out. Only the slaves were left behind to boil the body and clean up the mess. Dr. Hunter and William Hewson went over the highlights of the event together and eventually, the conversation steered toward an unexpected invitation.

"I have a meeting next week with a dear friend I would like to introduce you to. Perhaps you've heard of the inventor and states-man, Dr. Benjamin Franklin?"

Hewson was dumbstruck.

"Why, of course. I grew up on Poor Richard's Almanac. I've followed his work closely since I started working under Dr. Lambert at the Newcastle Infirmary."

"Ah yes, he and Dr. Lambert have been very close for a good many years," Hunter said.

"Yes, indeed. I have heard great tales of their exploits together in the pubs from Dr. Lambert himself," Hewson replied.

"Since Dr. Franklin moved to London he has been lodging at the home of my late colleague, Dr. Stevenson. I am sure you two will become fast friends."

CHAPTER 8

36 CRAVEN STREET

THE COACHMAN STOPPED his horses in front of the house at 36 Craven Street. It was a balmy night and Hewson and Dr. Hunter could see their hot breath piping as they walked up the steps to the red brick townhouse with a stone facade. Dr. Hunter lifted the brass lion head door knocker and rapped it three times. It was a surreal moment for Hewson. Here he was, about to walk into the home of a man whose myth so far preceded him, that he was timeless in his own day. Few living men possessed such a level of gravitas as the one he was about to meet. The thought of him in flesh-and-blood just beyond this door sent an uncontrollable shudder through Hewson's body and he became hyper-aware of his surroundings. It was as if time continued to exist only to monitor the progress of his bowels, which were quickening with excitement.

The door opened, revealing an African slave dressed in formal attire. As he ushered the men inside it dawned on Hewson that this was the man from the Anatomical Society lecture who assisted him in hollowing out the corpse.

"Tis hard to find good negros these days," Hunter piped.

"Dr. Franklin generously lends me this one to assist in our lectures. His name is King."

The stoic King guided the men through the hall to the smoking room and motioned them inside with an outstretched hand. Hewson noticed one of King's long fingers was adorned by a beautiful emerald ring. In the smoking room, four large chairs sat facing one another before a grand hearth that housed a raging fire. Dr. Benjamin Franklin sat in one of the chairs, engaged in conversation with a young beauty sitting on his lap, her milky arms draped lazily around his neck while she gazed into the eyes of the speaking elder with admiration. Hewson could see he was intruding on a profound moment, though Franklin and the girl had yet to notice his presence.

"...and that my dear is infinite." Franklin finished, punctuating his remark with a tap on the girl's slightly upturned, freckled nose. King cleared his throat and the girl jumped to her feet a little embarrassed while Franklin grabbed ahold of his cane and leaned heavily on it to help him stand.

"Dr. Hunter, it is so good to see you again," he chimed with the fire of mirth glowing brightly in his eyes.

"You as well, Dr. Franklin," laughed Dr. Hunter.

Franklin reached for Hunter's hand and shook it tightly, then his gaze shifted toward Hewson who had just finished exchanging blushing glances with the pretty blonde girl.

"This is my protege, Dr. William Hewson."

"Ah, yes the young blood expert," Franklin's fiery eyes looked into Hewson's soul and drank him in. "I am aware of your fascinating work with reptiles at the Newcastle Infirmary under my dear old friend, Sir Richard Lambert."

Franklin took Hewson's hand in his thick paw and shook it with a strength that woke the young surgeon up. All went silent and almost black for a moment as the blood rushed to Hewson's head. He could not believe it—his idol knew his work.

"This is Mary," Franklin said, introducing the beauty.

"However, I call her Polly. I also call her my daughter."

"How do you do, madam."

"Very fine, thank you…and you too may call me Polly."

Knives sliced into pheasants on silver plates along a candlelit table as the diners laughed and talked gaily over supper that night. The volume of conversation grew louder as the night wore on and King kept the wine flowing into their cups. Hewson noticed there was no meat on Franklin's plate, only the vegetarian sides: boiled potatoes, peas, dried cranberries, and a big slice of buttered bread.

"So, tell me more about this new anatomical society you are running hidden amongst the derelicts of Gin Lane," Franklin said.

"Since neither the University, nor the Church, and therefore, the Law, supports our kind of endeavor, we have endeavored to take endeavors into our own hands," Hunter said.

The table enjoyed a heady laugh at Hunter's reply. The wine was loosening him up and he was finding his stride. In fact, all of the diners were becoming lighter in spirit and redder in the face. Franklin's landlady–and Polly's mother–the Widow Mrs. Stevenson, laughed a little too loud for a little too long. Hewson and Polly blushed at each other across the table.

"Hewson has been a Godsend. He shall become the leading scholar in the study of the blood, this much I know to be true," Hunter proclaimed.

Franklin pierced Hewson with hungry eyes.

"Yes, I can tell Dr. Hewson is a man of great potential. I recognize that sort of thing the moment I see it."

"Thank you, sir," Hewson stated with a slight bow.

An old hunched-over slave woman from the kitchen hobbled toward a strange and beautiful instrument that looked like a giant glass carrot. She turned a crank that started it spinning,

"The Glass Armonica," Franklin said. "One of my inventions.

The instrument is a series of glass bowls stacked inside of one another, large descending to small, and secured horizontally to spinning mechanical wheels made of wood and brass on either side. Mima plays it beautifully."

Mima wet her knobby, arthritic fingers in a small bowl of water and applied them to the spinning Glass Armonica, producing wavy, ethereal tones. King made his rounds filling the diner's cups, his emerald ring shining under Dr. Hunter's eyes.

"I say, Ben, you really do have the most attentive negros. We could not have done without the help of King during our surgery yesterday."

King shot a glance in Franklin's direction.

"Yes. King is invaluable," Franklin said.

The old widow beckoned the dignified slave to her aid. She was deep in her cups.

"More wine, King. More wine," she said.

King filled the drunken widow's glass with stoic condemnation. After a long pour, he corked the bottle with a tight squeak.

Franklin pipped, "Wine is constant proof that God loves us and loves to see us happy," and the diners laughed.

After dinner, the men sat by the fire in velvet chairs smoking long pipes. King filled their glasses with sherry while they talked and smoked. All were quite drunk by now.

"I shall be frank," Franklin stated. "I support what you men are doing and should like to be involved in any way that I can. I have always been fascinated by the study of anatomy. Tis' a shame society has not yet caught up with our much-maligned science," he concluded with an air of sadness.

"We should like to have you down to view our surgery. We are having one next week," Hunter said.

"Indeed, I accept," Franklin said, then squared his gaze on Hewson once again. "Tell me more about your study of the blood."

"Well, I am presently entranced by the process of coagulation," Hewson said. "It has occupied me for some months and I suspect I am finally on the verge of a major breakthrough."

Franklin nodded with sympathetic, energetic eyes, despite his ruddy face.

"You remind me of myself in my youth. Utterly gripped by a fascination to know all I could about life and the hidden mechanics of the world," he said.

Hewson listened while the Master spoke.

"I can see the obsession in you. The desire to thwart the Grim Reaper with the Philosopher's Stone."

Hewson acknowledged Franklin's statement with a polite laugh. He had never thought of it that way, but Franklin certainly was not wrong.

"Yes, I suppose that is a fair assessment," Hewson allowed.

Franklin continued, "We have a fierce dissatisfaction with accepting the material realm as it appears. I share your renegade thirst to understand mortality by any means necessary."

The polymath stopped short of licking his chops.

CHAPTER 9

BEN FRANKLIN IN YOUTH

WILLIAM HEWSON, THE promising young surgeon, had ignited Franklin's memory, sending him on a trip down the river of time, all the way back to his colonial youth in Boston, Massachusetts where he lived with his parents and sixteen siblings, all crammed into a small country home. In 1720, when Franklin was a young man, he spent the warmer months giving swimming lessons to the local children in the Charles River. He had even come up with a wooden paddle device that strapped to the swimmer's hands to help propel them forward through the water like fins do for a fish. The wooden swimming paddles were one of Franklin's earliest inventions. To his mother it seemed as if Ben had walked out of her womb with an active mind, searching, probing, turning every moment around to examine all of it from all sides. He had the mind of a genius from the beginning–a naturalist with a most insatiable curiosity. However, his parents did not always view his curiosity as a praise-worthy quality. It was a cause for alarm–a sign that their son was not well. When Ben was only nine years old, he invented a cage with a booby-trapped door for trapping small animals. He used this device to trap a rabbit in the forest, which he hid behind a tree until he came back under the cover of night to retrieve and sneak down to the basement by the light of an oil lamp. Once safe inside the basement, he pulled the big floppy rabbit out of the cage and came down hard on the poor creature's head with a ball-peen hammer, then proceeded to dissect it. He pulled out its innards and studied every organ, then commenced to sketch diagrams in his little paper journal. Ben was in the beginning stages of his fascination with anatomy, however, this was the only instance of his prolific experiments that his parents were aware of. After documenting his own process so carefully, this journal fell into the hands of his older brother James, who never missed an opportunity to humiliate young Ben. James possessed a fierce jealousy of his little brother's brilliant mind and natural talents. Ben's achievements far surpassed anything James was capable of, though he was ten years the boy's senior. James ran a print shop in town, but still nothing was as impressive as his wunderkind brother. At the breakfast table the morning after the rabbit experiment, James stood and shouted over the rabble of chaotic conversation happening between his parents and sixteen brothers and sisters.

"I have an announcement to make!"

The conversations halted at once in the wake of this bizarre interruption. To Ben's horror, James pulled the small paper journal from his pants pocket.

"The sneaky bastard," Ben thought as he sank in his chair.

James cleared his throat and opened the journal to Ben's sketches of the rabbit made during dissection the night before, the pages still sticky with fresh blood.

"We have a great anatomist in our midst—Benjamin Franklin!" he announced.

James offered to present Ben with an outstretched arm, which his little brother declined, instead slumping further down into his chair. James passed the journal to his sister Sarah, who covered her mouth in shock then passed it on to her sister Lydia, who did the same, passing the journal to Hannah, who was giggling maniacally all along, until she viewed the disturbing illustrations that caused her to choke on her own refuse. Hannah passed the journal to Jane, who passed it to Anne, Mary, and all of the brothers, while Ben's mother jolted to her feet and seized Ben's ear. She dealt her punishments swiftly, lest raising a brood of seventeen leave time for nothing else. When there was a disruption, it had to be stopped right away. She dragged the offender by the ear onto the back patio to the sound of his siblings' laughter.

"If you can find a rabbit to rip apart in those woods, surely you can find a switch thick enough for me to beat you with."

She kicked Ben in the ass as he walked off the porch into the woods to select the switch with which he would be beaten. His mother was a hard woman.

Ben spent a lot of time in the woods, climbing trees and exploring. He was an athletic boy, and he grew into a strapping young man. Swimming seemed to be the only activity that could quiet his busy mind, if only for a moment. He loved the sport and in the warmer months, he took every opportunity to get into the water. The Franklin home was only a hop and a skip away from the Charles River, which was convenient for the young swimmer. By the time Ben turned fifteen, he was giving lessons to all of the local kids. His congregation grew to include thirty-five youths in the high season. This was in part due to Ben's charisma and passion for the sport, but also, because of his wild inventions. He came up with paddles that acted as flippers like one might find on a fish, helping propel the swimmers through the water with speed and vigor. The oval paddles strapped to the hands of the swimmer with a leather band. The kids loved using them. One summer, Ben found that most of his free time outside of giving lessons and reading was devoted to whittling more of these paddles as his class grew. However, Ben's passion for the other sciences never waned. He was still hopelessly curious about anatomy.

One particular summer day, Ben had just concluded a strenuous class teaching the "butterfly" swim when he noticed a young native boy around his age watching him from the forest. Ben was all the way down the hill, on the bank of the river collecting coins from his clients as they filed out with their hand paddles. The young native was curious about Ben and the kids and wondered if they were friendly. Perhaps he too could join in their sport? The young native waited until all of the other kids were gone before coming out from behind the trees. Ben made his way up closer to the tree line as the young native emerged. The two boys approached each other with caution, feeling each other out. Eventually, the native boy approached Ben and presented him with a decorated bone knife balanced on his fingers by the blade and handle. Ben took the knife and stabbed the boy to death with it before he knew what happened. He straddled the boy's bloody body on the forest floor and flayed his chest wide open with the sharp knife, reached inside of his chest cavity, and pulled out his beating heart. Ben studied it closely, watching the pulse slow to a stop. When he was finished, he dragged the boy's corpse down the hill and into the Charles River, like an alligator with its prey. Then, he washed the blood off of his body, scrubbing hard as the sun began to set. His mother would kill him if she noticed his blood-stained hands.

One may find it surprising that the man who went on to write the famous "Thirteen Virtues," along with a prolific collection of essays and letters on morality had such a checked record as a youth. Being one of seventeen children, Ben grew up rather poor. His mother and father could not spare the expense to lend him a few cents to purchase books at the rate his active mind hungered to consume them. As a teenager, he became a vegetarian in order to save every penny to buy books and to help fund his many experiments. Ever resourceful, the youth sometimes resorted to less honest means to get what he needed. It is also surprising to learn that the book he stole that had the biggest impact on his life's trajectory was not of Platonic philosophy or Christian teachings, but of ancient magic and occult wisdom traditions. Ben was a frequent customer at the Old Corner Book Store in downtown Boston. Sometimes he paid and sometimes he didn't, depending on whether or not he could afford his current obsession. One day while scanning the isles of old religious texts, his eye was caught by the beautiful gold-gilt lettering on an old leather bound book entitled *Ancient Wisdom And Magic*. When he pulled it off the shelf, he saw to his wonder and amazement, a golden triangle with a single eye at the center and shining sun rays emanating from behind. He had to have it. He looked around, slid the book into his overcoat, and slipped out the door. That afternoon, James snuck up on his little brother whose nose was deep in the mysterious book. He demanded to know where it came from, knowing his cunning little brother must have stolen it from somewhere. The two engaged in a powerful tug-o-war, but Ben was stronger than his scrawny older brother. He ripped the book away from James and spanked him hard over the head with it, telling him to, "piss off!"

The two brothers quarreled endlessly in their youth. Even so, out of all his siblings Ben was closest with James. After all, it was James who gave Ben a job at his print shop and taught him the craft that would become his first and arguably most important trade–printing and publishing. It was printing that would ignite Ben's legacy as a writer and spread his musings to the colonies through his annual hit publication, *Poor Richard's Almanac*. But even this he stole from James, who first printed the concept unsuccessfully as *Poor Robin's Almanac*. Ben had a flair for tenacious marketing and he was simply a better writer than his older brother. He knew how to self-promote, unlike James, who was afraid to put himself out in the public eye. Also, Ben had no qualms with resorting to nefarious means to get the results he desired. His craving for public attention was often a greater driving force than his powerful curiosity. The desire for fame. The desire to be known. The desire to become a man of great importance.

Although the brothers bickered they were both hard workers and dedicated to their craft. However, Ben's extracurricular affairs sometimes caught up with him at the workplace. Along with his insatiable curiosity, he had a powerful sex appetite. One day, a girlfriend of Ben's showed up to the print shop brandishing a stash of love letters. She stormed in on the Franklin brothers setting type fonts.

"My sister, Ben?" she cried. The buxom young beauty threw the letters in his face and took off sobbing with a ding of the doorbell shouting, "Bastard!"

James clapped Ben's ears for that one.

"Tell your girlfriends to quit coming around here lest all of Philadelphia mistake my print shop for a brothel!"

From Ben's point of view, the sex was always worth the trouble. He loved a good conquest and sometimes he chose the easier path by satiating the primal urge with his weekly wages at the local whorehouse. That same night, in a heavily velveted room lit by a glowing red lantern, Ben stood before three of Philadelphia's finest whores.

"I want them all," he said and handed the madam a satchel of coins.

By the time Ben received a letter from London that would forever change the course of his life, he had been working under James for several years and had mastered the art of printing. Some months earlier in the spring of 1724, Ben sent a letter to the most highly-regarded printer in London, James Watts, seeking an apprenticeship. Still unknown, with hardly any professional career to speak of, young Ben thrust his correspondence out into the darkness knowing he would get the response he desired...and he did. Ben was at his workstation that morning setting fonts in the typeform for the evening news when the postman arrived with the ding of a bell.

"A letter from London addressed to a Mr. Franklin," the postman said.

Both Ben and James raised their heads at this unusual interruption. Ben broke the wax seal and unfolded the letter to reveal a note in grand, artfully arranged print.

FROM THE OFFICE OF JAMES WATTS, PRINTER ESQ.

Ben had been patiently awaiting this pleasant moment for months, a moment which his brother James had no idea was coming.

"I have been accepted," the smug Ben stated.

"What?" James asked, "How?"

"I have been accepted to an apprenticeship with James Watts," Ben said.

James' blood was steadily boiling. "The London printer James Watts?" he queried.

"Yes, the London printer James Watts. Is there any other?" Ben replied with a smirk.

James threw his fonts down on the typeform and went straight for Ben's neck, choking him in a rage. Ben broke his brother's hold and soon the two were locked in a violent tussle, a lifelong feud coming to a head. They banged into a large wooden and glass case of carefully organized fonts which came crashing to the ground sending tiny metal fonts bouncing all over the floor. They smashed into the typesetter, destroying their laborious day's work. Soon, the stronger Ben gained the upper hand. He grabbed James by his colonial ponytail, then by the neck, and smashed his face down on the printing press typeform. Ben grabbed a hold of a large wooden lever and pulled down, pressing James' face between the typeform and the plate and causing him to shriek in pain. James' red face looked as though it might pop from such a powerful squeeze and Ben relished the thought, but decided to spare his brother so that he might live with the shame of now *knowing* he had been bested in every way by his younger brother. Ben released the lever and James fell to the floor with the daily news imprinted on his face.

"I am going to London," Ben said, breathing heavily with excitement.

Within a day Ben found himself at the Philadelphia Seaport Delaware River Anchorage where the towering transatlantic vessel, *The London Hope*, awaited boasting several flags on high masts blowing in the crisp morning wind as a sea of passengers shuffled up the ramp and into her carriage like an army of ants. Ben joined the line, holding his every possession before him in a large trunk made of leather and wood. It was not much, but then again, he did not need much in those lean days. A couple of suits, his journal, quill, and inkwell, and the only book he owned that truly mattered to him—*Ancient Wisdom And Magic*. Every piece of "luck" in his life could be traced directly to what he had learned in this book, which among other things, included the powerful sorcery of manifesting one's desires by envisioning them clearly and knowing it to be reality. He imagined himself receiving his acceptance as he wrote his letter of application to James Watts. He imagined boarding a vessel to London and becoming a successful printer and highly respected author and publisher in Europe. He knew there was nothing in this life he could not have if he wanted it and that he was an active participant in sculpting his future in images on the wall of his conscious mind. A string quartet played "Water Music" by Handel as the passengers boarded, including a few rats and a few cats scurrying up the plank and into a porthole on the side of the ship. Seeing the rats scurry made Ben aware of a powerful itch in his groin followed by a burning desire to urinate. He managed to get on board and bring his trunk to his bed before going down to the ship infirmary, all before wetting himself. Ben had experienced the pox before and already knew he needed a mercury shot, fast. He was all but drenched in fever sweat by the time he sat on a stool in the office of a rather stout and rotund Welsh physician in the ship's underbelly. The physician took one look at the shivering Ben and filled a large brass syringe with liquid mercury from a glass apothecary vial.

"Aye, so a nice little bobtail peppered your pego. Not so nice after all, was she?" said the Welshman, chuckling to himself as he filled his syringe with quicksilver. Ben did not find him funny.

"You know what they say. Spend one night with Venus and get a week with Mercury."

The chubby doctor stuck the needle in Ben's arm and pressed down hard on the plunger sending in a painful shot of sludgy quicksilver that caused instant and profuse salivation.

"Takin' it like a pro," said the Welshman.

Unenthused, Ben cocked his head toward the physician, as a constant stream of thick saliva poured from his mouth straight down to the floor.

"I can see this is not your first time," the Welshman said with an exaggerated wink.

During those first weeks at sea, Ben suffered the pox but he took several shots of poisonous heavy metals that drove the sickness from his constitution. Eventually, his fever passed and he was able to focus enough to write in his leather bound journal. Surrounded by other lower-class passengers, Ben sat upright in his bunk writing an entry with his feather quill and inkwell.

NOVEMBER 26TH, 1724

DAY 21. TWO OF THE ELDERLY HAVE DIED. MY CONDITION HAS IMPROVED BUT I FEAR THAT MADNESS IS LOOMING ON MY HORIZON. HOW WILL I LAST ANOTHER WEEK ON THIS GODFORSAKEN VESSEL?

Just then a rat ran alongside the railing of his bunk and stopped long enough to lock eyes before scurrying along to its destination. Suddenly, an unsightly passenger woman fell to the ground, convulsing. Ben watched as a commotion began to rise among his fellow passengers. The Welsh physician appeared and dragged the woman away to be treated. Would she make it? Or would she wind up under a linen blanket in the death room with the elderly who passed earlier that week? Ben assumed the latter was most likely. Though she was on the younger side she did not look healthy. After some time had passed, Ben made his way down to the death room to confirm his suspicion. After looking around with caution to make sure that pesky Welshman was nowhere to be seen, Ben entered and approached the third mound of white linen heaped on a tabletop beside two others. He peeled back the linen, revealing the bloated, naked body of the woman who had shook so violently on the bunkroom floor just an hour or two earlier. Looking around once more, Ben unbuckled his kickers.

Later that afternoon, Ben sat in his bunk working on another entry.

SILENCE. AVOID TRIFLING CONVERSATION.

ORDER. LET EACH PART OF YOUR BUSINESS HAVE ITS TIME.

CHASTITY. WHEN YOU USE VENERY, MAKE IT COUNT.

CHAPTER 10

THE LONDON STATESMAN

THE YEAR OF Our Lord, 1770. Elites of the Georgian London intelligentsia gather at The King's Arms tavern to drink and daunt the deep-cleavaged waitresses with drunken stares and thinly veiled innuendo. It is a raucous place where men drink porter from pewter tankards and debate whether passion or reason governs human behavior. The kind of place where fisticuffs are not uncommon over the course of an afternoon or evening. Benjamin Franklin–the Ambassador of the American Colonies to Great Britain–now well into his seventies with white hair hanging down to his shoulders, is as active as ever, politically, socially, and in his private studies. He is drinking at a table engaged in a chaotic discussion with several politicians including Sir Fletcher Norton–a fat, mean-looking man with furrowed eyebrows and long, bulbous white hair, and Edmund Burke–a fat, pasty Irishman with concerned, beady eyes and shorter red hair.

The Irishman Edmund Burke breaks into the conversation.

"Let us drink and dine well today, gentleman, for tomorrow blood will spill on the floor of the House Of Commons," he slurred.

The men at the table laugh. Ben Franklin offers a retort.

"Yes, but not as much as will spill in America if the Crown thinks she can tax the Colonists beyond her due share."

The men let out various exclamations at this controversial statement.

"Aye, I knew the man was a dirty spy!" someone shouted.

"In all of the vast forests and plains of America, you will never encounter a man whose wit and grace can match the sharp mind of a commoner on this small stretch of island we call England," said Franklin.

Some of the men chuckle and others grumble.

"I will drink to that!" says one of the lesser politicians.

"Do you pretend to believe this insincere rake?" the former dissident asks.

Franklin makes a further effort to lighten the mood.

"No, no it is true! My love for Old England is deep, however, this does not negate my responsibility to the Colonists. After all, I am here to represent them," he said.

"Yes and we shall test your mettle before the House Of Commons the morrow," said Burke, the ruddy-faced Irishman.

"It won't be the first time and I am sure it will not be the last," Franklin said and all of the men chuckled.

"Indeed Dr. Franklin, I look forward to a healthy, rigorous debate," said the mean-faced Sir Fletcher Norton who raised his pewter than took a mouthful of porter.

The next day the men appear in a meeting before the House Of Commons to debate a new tax set to be imposed upon the American Colonies. Golden framed paintings line the towering green walls under a half-dome ceiling with a planetary curve. Sir Fletcher Norton presides from his wooden throne. The Members of Parliament sit in chairs behind which stands a crowd of lords, ladies, lesser politicians, courtesans, and clergy. Sir Fletcher Norton calls Dr. Benjamin Franklin before the assembly and begins the inquisition.

"Do the Americans pay considerable taxes among themselves?" he asks.

"Certainly many, and very heavy taxes," Franklin replies.

"Do you think it right that America should be protected by this country and pay no part of the expense?"

"That is not the case. The Colonies raised, clothed, and paid, during the last war, nearly 25,000 men, and spent many millions."

"Do you not think the people of America would submit to pay the proposed stamp tax?"

"No, never. Not unless compelled by force of arms."

Later that night, Ben Franklin and Erasmus Darwin sit face-to-face in a dark room, a single flame burning between them being their only light. Darwin holds a handful of letters.

"The time has come for the final act, Judas," he says to Franklin.

"I have here some incendiary letters between the Crown and the Governor of Massachusetts that will indeed widen the breach."

He hands the letters to Franklin.

"See to it that these are published in the Boston press," Darwin commands.

CHAPTER 11

THE CANDIDATE

HEWSON WAS BUSY at work in Dr. William Hunter's home laboratory, dissecting a human lymph node on a white oriental porcelain platter using two small scalpels. He sliced a thin piece away from one of the nodes and placed it on the glass of a wood and brass microscope, then looked under the viewfinder to find a dazzling tapestry of pink orbs milling about. Dr. Hunter entered unable to hide his concern and suspicion as to the contents of the letter he held in his hand.

"How are your studies on the lymphatic system coming along?" he queried.

"Very well," said Hewson while adjusting the focus on the microscope.

"I am beginning to see how the lymph nodes filter blood."

Hewson picked his quill out of the inkwell and wrote in his journal.

THE LYMPHATIC FLUID

Dr. Hunter pressed forward, clearing his throat. With some

hesitancy, he said, "Good. I have here a letter addressed to you from Dr. Franklin."

Hewson put the quill back in the inkwell and wiped the blood from his hands with a handkerchief. Dr. Hunter handed him the letter and he used his scalpel to break the wax seal that said B.F. in old English writing and opened the letter.

"It is an invitation to dinner," said Hewson quite astonished, unable to hide his excitement.

Dr. Hunter stood with his back to Hewson looking out the window and said nothing.

At 36 Craven Street, knives sliced into pheasants on silver platters. Again, Franklin's plate contained only steamed vegetables and buttered bread. King kept the wine flowing as Franklin, Hewson, Polly, and the Widow Mrs. Stevenson conversed, dined, and drank. Hewson and Polly couldn't help shooting flirtatious glances across the table at each other. Franklin chewed his food slowly and deliberately, speaking while chewing but being careful not to be rude or gross about it.

"I ceased eating flesh as a young man, probably ten or so years younger than you are now," he said to Hewson, who was politely chewing a bit of pheasant.

"I see," replied Hewson. "I find it interesting, if I may say so. I do not think I have met someone who does not eat meat."

"We are an uncommon breed," Franklin said as he took a bite of boiled potato.

"The Jains in India have been vegetarian since ancient times, as part of their religion," said Polly.

She had been waiting for the right chance to join the conversation and this was it. She knew a thing or two about ancient cultures and relished in showing off her knowledge to Hewson.

"Certain Greek mystics did as well during Classical Antiquity.

They called their diet "abstinence from beings with a soul," she continued.

"Yes, well my reasons were far more practical," Franklin said, returning some levity to the conversation. "I was poor and needed money to buy books!"

Everyone at the table enjoyed a heady chuckle, especially the Widow Mrs. Stevenson, who always indulged her laughter for a bit longer than socially normal. King's emerald ring sparkled in the candlelight as he refilled the Widow's glass.

"What a magnificent ring," Hewson thought.

The merrymakers made merry. Gaiety hung in the air.

"My refusing to eat flesh occasioned an inconvenience, and I was frequently chided for my singularity, but I found I enjoyed greater clearness of head and quicker comprehension. I adopted the personal belief that flesh-eating is unprovoked murder…as opposed to provoked murder, which is perfectly all right."

Franklin's wit and charm elicited a big laugh from the heads at the table. Again, the Widow Mrs. Stevenson indulged in her laughter, drooling a little bit of red wine into her lap."

"Whoops!" she cried.

The hunchbacked slave woman hobbled over to the glass armonica, cranked it spinning, wet her fingers in the bowl, and began to play a piece from "Water Music" by Handel in glassy, ethereal tones.

After dinner, Franklin and Hewson sat in velvet chairs smoking long pipes beside a roaring fire.

"How did you get started in this business, anyhow?" Franklin asked with a puff on his pipe.

"Well, it was my twin sister," said Hewson. "She died from bad blood when we were children. She suffered terribly and nobody could help her. From that day on I have sensed it is my obligation to know all I can about the blood. No one should have to suffer that way, especially a child."

Franklin nodded, like an understanding friend or long lost uncle.

"A worthy cause, indeed. Has your stint working under Dr. Hunter shed some light on your studies?" he asked.

"Yes, a great deal of light. Dr. Hunter has afforded me, in addition to room and board, the opportunity to go from experimenting on turtles to working with real human cadavers. I am finally beginning to understand how blood behaves within the human body. Of course, since we are working with cadavers I must still rely on a certain amount of speculation, but my educated guesses have been greatly reduced," explained Hewson.

"Yes, there can be no substitute for working with a real human body when it comes to the study of anatomy,"

Franklin said, as he hit the pipe then released a large plume of smoke. "I for one am interested in locating the home of the human soul."

Being ever polite, Hewson chuckled, humoring the smiling Franklin.

"Descartes believed the soul of man lives in the pineal gland, behind the forehead," he contributed.

"Yes, and I intend to find out," said Franklin, deadly earnest.

King refilled their glasses as they paused a moment to enjoy the blazing fire. Franklin broke the long silence.

"I should like to be forthright with you, Mr. Hewson. I want you to be my protege."

Hewson could not believe his ears. He hung on Franklin's every word. The old Master continued,

"It will be a much smaller operation than Hunter's anatomy school and not open to the Society fellows, for the purpose of exploring our own studies, uninhibited. I will also offer you room and board here. You can further your study of the blood. I shall busy myself with mapping the human soul. You can understand why unlocking these mysteries must be kept secret."

Hewson nodded. "I am deeply honored, Dr. Franklin," he said. "But how will I tell Dr. Hunter? He has been so good to me. Without him, I would still be working with reptiles."

"I will work it out with him personally," Franklin said. "Dr. Hunter and I have known each other for a long time."

Hewson gave a mild show of being torn but inside he was giddy with excitement at the idea of living and working with the great Dr. Benjamin Franklin. This was a dream come true.

"Indeed, I humbly accept your generous offer Dr. It would be my pleasure to live and work under your guidance. I consider it the highest honor," said Hewson.

"Tell me," Franklin said. "Have you been to a hanging?"

CHAPTER 12

THE BODYSNATCHERS

FRANKLIN AND HEWSON found themselves among a large crowd gathered before the gallows in the city square. Nobleman, dirty peasants, flamboyant macaroni youth, syphilis drunks—all waiting to be entertained as if the hanging were a Roman gladiatorial event. The motley crowd erupted in a loud cheer as the condemned man ascended the steps to the gallows platform. There he was greeted by a tall hangman standing beside the swaying noose wearing a pointed black hood and robe.

"Thirteen steps to the gallows. Thirteen loops to the noose. He should have practiced the thirteen virtues!" Franklin shouted in Hewson's ear with a chuckle.

Only the burning eyes of the hangman could be seen shining from behind his black hood. The roar of the savage crowd grew louder as the hangman slipped the noose over the condemned man's head. Then the executioner threw up his hands signaling the crowd to silence.

"For committing the Carnal Sin of Adultery. Have you anything to say?" boomed the hangman from behind his sharp black hood.

"Who hasn't fucked around a little bit here and there?" said the condemned man with a pirate grin.

The crowd roared as the platform opened and the he dropped to his death, swaying to and fro with the creaking of wood and rope. The roar of the crowd soon turned to laughter then settled down to polite applause and light conversation as the hangman's slaves lowered the body from the gallows and onto a wooden cart, then moved out toward the River Thames.

"Don't lose that cart!" Franklin shouted in Hewson's ear.

The young surgeon took off on a mad scramble through the slowly dispersing crowd toward the River Thames. He knew from his time working with Dr. Hunter that this is the way things went. The hangman's slaves supplied the bodysnatchers with fresh corpses, for a fee of course. The bodysnatchers then supplied the anatomists with bodies for a pretty penny along with some danger to their life. The bodysnatchers were a criminal class of drunken pirates and were often known to knife their clients in paranoid delusions and rageful transactions. They were not a friendly crowd—the profession was rife with mistrust and dirty dealings. When Hewson arrived at the riverside he saw some of the same bodysnatchers he had known when picking up bodies with Dr. Hunter. Though his former mentor was a well-respected and frequent customer, Hewson had never dealt with the bodysnatchers on his own. The bodysnatchers took the body from the hangman's slaves, tossed them a shilling or two for their troubles, then dropped it in the boat. Careful to wait until the deal was done, Hewson made his approach before another anatomist who was possibly lurking somewhere could beat him to it. As he approached the boat the fat bodysnatcher became alarmed and grabbed Hewson's hair from behind. Holding the surgeon's head in arm lock he then put a knife to his throat while the others gathered around.

"Do you not remember me?" Hewson choked.

"That's the doctor's boy. Let him go," said the gaunt one with hardly any teeth. Disappointed, the fat bodysnatcher released Hewson.

"I need to purchase a body," Hewson explained.

Leaning over the bank and into the boat he could see there were two bodies lying under a dirty woolen blanket. The gaunt bodysnatcher peeled back the blanket to reveal the corpse of the condemned man and the body of a teenage girl, her eye holes squirming with maggots. Hewson gagged at the sight.

"Gonna cost extra for the freshie," said the gaunt bodysnatcher.

"He'll fetch a pretty penny," the fat one chimed in.

"I'll take the fresh one," said Hewson.

After a brief exchange of money, Hewson wheeled the blanket-covered corpse through the stony streets the grey sky faded into dusk. By the time he reached the alley behind 36 Craven Street, night had fallen. Once outside the back gate, Hewson let out a reserved whistle, to no effect. He gave a cautious but louder whistle. Nothing still. Hewson put both of his fingers in his mouth and blew with all his power. In the second-story window, a lit lantern flame began to glow. Soon after, Franklin appeared in the backyard and let Hewson through the gate. Lighting the way with his burning oil lamp, Franklin led his protege to a flowerbed of thriving red and white rosebushes. He stopped and bent over to grab a large brass ring in the grass beside the flowerbed. A trap door! He opened it and dangled the lantern inside for Hewson to see the steep wooden staircase that descended to a dirt floor below.

"I am afraid at my age I am no good for lifting heavy things," Franklin said.

Mustering all of his strength, Hewson managed to hoist the body from the cart onto his back. Franklin went down the steps first, lighting the way as Hewson followed shakily, grunting and groaning under the dead weight of the body. Once inside, Franklin lit the way to a wooden table on which Hewson flopped the body with a thud, barely making it. Franklin lit several dripping wax candles on the table that partially illuminated his makeshift laboratory. Then he lit an oil lamp sitting on a shelf beside many aqua glass mason jars which appeared to house strange organs floating in some kind of transparent liquid. Many of the jars were empty. There was also a collection of apothecary flasks filled with clear and amber liquids. The laboratory was a total mess, compared to Dr. Hunter's, Hewson though. Franklin grabbed one of the empty mason jars, set it on the table beside the body, and unscrewed the lid. He then selected one of the corked clear liquid flasks and set it beside the mason jar. Hewson noticed a strange stone box looming in the corner of the room.

"What is *that*?" he thought.

Franklin unrolled a cloth that contained several scalpels out onto the table beside the body and his flasks. A crude drill of iron, brass, and wood hung on the wall beside the shelf of jars. Franklin took it off the nail.

"Never leave that till tomorrow which you can do today," he said as he stuck the trepanning device to the man's forehead and began to drill, sending up a dark pool of blood like oil pouring from the earth.

Following Franklin's lead Hewson went to work. He located a wooden bucket, placed it at the foot of the table. He selected a scalpel from Franklin's cloth and sliced the bottom of each foot, bleeding the man out into the bucket. Next, he sliced a line from the groin to the chin. Franklin was still drilling away at the head. He had now reached the skull and was crankling with gusto, grunting through the stubborn part. Having gone far enough, he reversed the crank until the drill was out of the man's head. He set the gory object down on the operating table. Hewson watched as Franklin squished his forefinger and thumb into the forehead, dug out the little almond-shaped pineal gland, and placed it in the open mason jar. With his bloody, brainy hand, Franklin popped the flask open and poured the clear liquid over the pineal gland, then corked the flask with a squeak and screwed the lid onto the mason jar. Hewson gripped the corpse's ribcage with both hands and cracked it wide open. He cut out the heart and placed it on the tabletop. Next, he sliced out a string of lymph nodes from the neck and placed it beside the heart.

The blood-splattered men looked at each other, their chests heaving with the excitement of the shared experience.

Later that night, by the light of an oil lantern, Hewson stood in a clawfoot tub scrubbing away the blood with a sponge and a bucket of sudsy water. With his hair slicked back and wet, he sat at his desk to elaborate on his notes made during the surgery. The pages of his notebook contained smeared, blood-splattered sketches of organs made hastily while the body was still on the table. Hewson studied them to decipher what he was seeing in the heat of the surgery that he had tried to capture. He wrote in his journal:

THE LYMPHATIC SYSTEM – RECENT FINDINGS

His writing was interrupted by a knock on the door. Was Franklin really coming to his room this late at night? Maybe there was something from the surgery he wished to discuss at once, Hewson thought. He opened the door to find Polly, wearing only a thin nightgown.

"What are you doing here?" he asked.

"I came to see you, nincompoop," replied Polly.

Hewson was stunned. She pushed him into the room, stepped inside, and shut the door.

CHAPTER 13

THE INITIATE

INSIDE OF A dark room, a single candle burned between two faces in profile. Franklin's face in silhouette spoke to that of a mysterious man.

"I have heard there is a place down on Gin Lane where godless men dissect human bodies," Franklin said.

"Aye," replied the stranger.

Soon, an angry mob carrying torches stormed the nighttime streets of Gin Lane, passing syphilitic skeletons sucking on bottles of gin on balconies, in the gutters, puking and brawling, fighting for their lives, paying little mind to the torch-carrying mob headed for the Windmill Street Anatomical Theatre of Dr. William Hunter. Hunter stood in front of the building holding the door open for his new protege, a young man who wheeled a corpse on a wooden cart into the lab. By the time the old surgeon saw them coming it was too late. The leader of the mob pointed him out.

"There's the ghoul!"

The mob broke into a run toward the anatomical theatre.

"Bodysnatcher!" one of them shouted.

Another man grabbed Hunter and held him from behind while the others threw glass bottles of kerosine into the lab, followed by their torches. Dr. Hunter could only watch in horror as his life's work went up in flames.

The next day, Ben Franklin and Erasmus Darwin walked London's grey, crowded streets with their skinny canes. A newsboy with a sack of rolled-up papers slung around his shoulder cried out the headlines:

"The American Colonists are crying for revolution! Riots in the Colonies against the Crown!"

Franklin gave the boy a coin in exchange for a paper. With Darwin at his side, he unrolled the paper.

COLONIAL REVOLT! HUTCHINSON LETTERS SPARK BOSTON RIOTS

"So mote it be," Franklin said.

"So mote it be," replied Darwin.

Lanterns and candles burning in wall sconces cast a warm glow over the dark wooden tables and benches of the King's Arms Tavern, which were presently filled with London's intellectual elite drinking themselves drunk on porter from pewter tankards. Red-faced politicians, clergymen, physicians, and many other professions argued philosophical points from across crowded tables. Rose of Chiswick, pink and fat as a country swine in his waistcoat and frilly shirt sat talking politics with the gaunt Burgh of Newington Green, the famous non-conformist.

"I do not care if they call me a second-class citizen," Burgh stated. "The Anglican Church can suckle me dongle."

"You are a fine specimen of a man. The landed gentry is honored to count you among our company," said Rose of Chiswick with pompous sarcasm.

"I am landed by ancestry, not by choice. The gentry is a lobcock! A big, floppy old lobcock!" Burgh shouted.

Rose of Chiswick blushed. He had nothing to say to that. Dr. Price, who writes on morals, leaned in, injecting himself into the conversation.

"The man stands to his guns," he slurred.

Benjamin Franklin entered the scene, followed by William Hewson. It was Hewson's first time at the famed Kings Arms Tavern and he was awestruck by the company in which he was now immersed. Rose of Chiswick banged upon the table, deeply enraged at Dr. Price, who, in return, banged upon the table. The philosopher David Hume sat with Erasmus Darwin, who spotted Franklin from across the room and beckoned him to their end of the table. The philosopher and the naturalist were smoking long pipes with John Temple, a keen supporter of a bill of rights for the American Colonists, and William Whately, the wealthy merchant politician. Franklin introduced Hewson to the group of raucous men. A deep-cleavaged barmaid came around with a sideboard of Welsh rabbits, apple puffs, and more porter. She sat two foamy pewter tankards down for the newcomers.

Franklin packed his pipe, lit it on a candle, and became immediately interested in an argument building between John Temple and William Whately. The latter stood from the table and leaned in close to Temple's face.

"Supporting independence for the American Colonists is an act of treason against the Crown of Mother England," he spewed, flipping Temple's porter pewter into his lap.

John Temple sprang to his feet, the crotch of his knickers soaked in porter. Everybody laughed, including Franklin, who was just getting into his cup.

"To Mother England!" Franklin shouted, raising his pewter.

"To Mother England!" shouted some of the others, raising their tankards and smashing them together.

"What about the American Colonies?" Whately shouted at Franklin, silencing the rabble. Suddenly, everyone in the bar was looking at them.

"May God bless them," Franklin replied. "Remember this–I am a Colonist, but first, I am a Briton."

Whately's temper rose by the second. He looked as though he might explode. In his fury, he shouted,

"The Colonists are rioting against the Crown! Have you not seen the papers? They are burning Hutchinson and Oliver in effigy on Boston Common!"

"That's enough, sir!" John Temple shouted, still dabbing at his soaked knickers with a handkerchief.

"Temple!" Whately pointed to the porter-soaked man. "John Temple incited this treason by giving private letters regarding Offical matters of the Crown to the Boston press for publication. You won't read about that in our papers!"

"Outrageous!" Temple threw his handkerchief on the table.

Whately offered a solution, swaying to and fro. "Perhaps a duel will settle the matter?" He said, relishing in his own brazen wit.

"Perhaps!" shouted Temple.

The learned men poured out of the tavern, cheering and jeering drunk. They loved a good duel.

Whately and Temple assumed their positions in the middle of the street as a crowd of onlookers gathered round.

Temple began to speak but Whately cut him off. "I will go first," he said, having just finished loading his pistol.

The crowd gasped as Whately raised his pistol at John Temple, who was still loading. He shot and missed drawing another loud gasp from the onlookers.

Having loaded his pops, Temple took aim and shot, popping a

hole in Whately's shoulder and sending him staggering backward with a mild grimace before he hit the ground, drawing yet another loud gasp from the crowd.

Seeking to lighten the mood, Erasmus Darwin pipped up. "'Tis' a good thing Dr. Franklin brought his surgeon friend along!"

Suddenly, everyone was looking at Hewson. Franklin chuckled and handed him a knife.

"Go on my boy," he said. "Show these rascals what you're made of."

Hewson straddled Whatley's body. Without thinking, he stuck the knife in the shoulder wound and popped out the musket ball, which bounced a few times before rolling away, drawing a loud cheer from the onlookers. Franklin and Darwin beamed with red-faced pleasure. Their boy Hewson had officially arrived.

The next afternoon found Franklin and Darwin walking with their skinny canes through London's grey stone streets crowded with dirty peasants, politicians, noblemen, and clergy. A sprinkling of skeletal tramps guzzled from mostly empty bottles of gin. A group of macaroni youth, in their towering white wigs, leopard fur knickers, and painted-up faces, shared a dull, airy laugh in unison, completely unenthused. Now sober, Franklin and Darwin discussed the grave events of the previous night at the Kings Arm's Tavern.

"There never was a revolution without a little bloodshed," Franklin stated.

"I believe the Colonists are prepared to go to war over this," replied Darwin.

"Yes, this and many other things. Tis' only the beginning," said Franklin.

"You truly possess the gift of saying a lot without saying what you really want to say," stated Darwin.

The men smiled at each other. Just a couple of high-ranking masons enjoying an afternoon stroll.

"A trick of the trade," said Franklin. "And I never lay brick without mortar."

"Prepare yourself, Judas. The Crown will attempt to destroy you," Darwin warned.

"Those who would give up Liberty, to purchase a little temporary Safety, deserve neither Liberty nor Safety," replied Franklin.

In the attic at 36 Craven Street, Hewson was busy humping Polly from behind against a dresser with a large attached mirror. The lusty lovers, mostly clothed, attempted to stifle their moans while getting off on their coital reflections in the mirror. One of Polly's breasts spilled out of her dress and exposed itself, prompting Hewson to withdraw and spend himself on the floor.

That night after dinner, Franklin and Hewson sat in tall velvet chairs beside the fire smoking long pipes. A strange gold amulet hung around Franklin's neck, bright against his white frilly shirt collar and grey vest. It was the "Eye Of Providence" situated inside of a triangle, like the ring that Dr. Richard Lambert used to wear. Hewson had not noticed such an amulet on Franklin, until now. He wondered what, if any, was the connection. Franklin burst his daydream with a startling question.

"What do you think of Polly?" He asked.

Hewson choked. "I beg your pardon?"

Franklin stared at him, saying nothing.

"She's a very nice girl. I think we get along fine," Hewson managed.

"Yes, and her womanhood is in full blossom. Is she not quite beautiful?" Franklin asked.

Hewson gave an awkward, polite smile.

Franklin pressed forward. "If a suitor should come along, I can only hope he be a man such as yourself. Strapping, handsome, brilliant. Highly capable."

A wave of relief began to wash over Hewson but Franklin continued,

"You see, Polly is like a daughter to me. I have watched her grow up all these years I have lived in London, away from my own children, who are now grown, too."

Hewson felt the muscles become tense around his bones again.

"It would simply break my heart to learn if Polly had been with a man before marriage," Franklin said, now staring into the fire.

"Why yes, of course," Hewson choked.

Franklin let the air out of the bag, knowing he had the boy where he wanted him.

"Ah, the sad musings of an old fool who misses his children. I do miss the Colonies as well," he said.

Hewson had no idea where this was going, but now, he could not allow himself to relax. Being in Franklin's presence was often like being on an old schooner tossed about on stormy seas.

"I have something for you," Franklin said. He produced a letter from his inner vest pocket and handed it to Hewson. The letter was sealed with a grand wax stamp which boasted the letters *A.P.S.*

"Go ahead," Franklin said. "Open it."

Hewson broke the wax seal and unfolded the letter. In classic colonial print, artfully arranged to take up the entire piece of paper, the text read:

TRANSACTIONS OF THE AMERICAN PHILOSOPHICAL SOCIETY HELD AT PHILADELPHIA, FOR PROMOTING USEFUL KNOWLEDGE.

Hewson flipped the letter over. In handwritten calligraphy, the beauty of which he had not seen until now, the heading read THE AMERICAN PHILOSOPHICAL SOCIETY...

"Read it out loud," Franklin urged.

Clearing his throat, Hewson continued, "Congratulations William Hewson. You have been elected as a member of the American Philosophical Society for scientific advancements in the study of the blood..."

Hewson looked to Franklin.

"Dr. Franklin, I am deeply honored but I'm afraid I do not quite understand. I have never even been to the colonies…"

Franklin interrupted. "We welcome worthy scholars to join our Society from the far reaches of the globe," he said.

Hewson let his guard down. He could not help it. A smile stretched across his face.

Franklin continued, "Our present membership includes the Prussian polymath Alexander von Humbolt, as well as Baron von Stueben, and the Marquis de Lafayette of France," Franklin chuckled. "I assure you, William, you are not alone."

"Well, thank you, sir. I humbly accept this invitation." Hewson felt at a loss for words. He was certain he was unworthy, yet he was profoundly excited. "From the depths of my soul, I owe you a debt of gratitude."

"Nonsense," stated Franklin. "But you do owe it to the Society to continue your study of the blood and to be a participating member, in good standing, by contributing your findings to our scholarly journal every now and again."

"Yes, absolutely," replied Hewson.

"If we are going to work together I need you to become more closely associated with my London colleagues," Franklin said.

Again, the young blood expert found himself at a loss for where the Old Master was going with all of this.

"I am part of a group of natural philosophers and thinkers. We call ourselves the Lunar Society because we meet every full moon at the Soho House of Erasmus Darwin."

Relishing the moment, Franklin took a long drag on his pipe then exhaled a billowy plume of smoke.

"We playfully refer to ourselves as *Lunaticks*."

A horse-drawn coach pulled up outside of 36 Craven Street where Franklin and Hewson stood waiting. The coachman opened the door for the gentlemen and they hoisted themselves inside, first Franklin, then Hewson. As the coachman closed the door, Franklin tied a blindfold around Hewson's eyes.

"'Tis' part of the romance," Franklin said.

The coach drove along a country path toward a full moon on a misty, magical horizon. After what seemed an eternity to Hewson, the coach pulled up in front of the Soho House of Erasmus Darwin. The coachman made haste around to the side and opened the door. He helped Hewson, who was still blindfolded, down as if he were a lady, followed by Franklin, violently puffing his pipe.

Franklin led the blindfolded Hewson through the house to an upstairs room. Several men sitting in velvet chairs holding lit, foot-long candles, craned their heads to view the late arrivals. Franklin and Hewson took their seats among them. Erasmus Darwin stood at the front of the room before an alter littered with dripping candles. A tray of surgical tools stood beside him—a scalpal, a pair of long tweezers, tiny sharp scissors, a neatly folded cloth rag.

"Judas," Darwin commanded. Hewson felt Franklin standing up beside him.

"Job."

Franklin placed his hand on Hewson's shoulder. He stood and Franklin escorted him to the front of the room, beside Darwin, the surgical tools, and the altar of dripping candles.

"Job, you may kneel before your master," Darwin said.

Hewson, aware that for some odd reason he was being referred to as Job, knelt. Darwin handed Franklin a piece of paper, yellowy-brown with age. Franklin held the paper in front of Hewson's blind-folded face.

"Job, remove the scales from your eyes," commanded Darwin.

Confused and hesitating, Hewson removed the blindfold. Many candle flames and strange faces came into focus, along with the piece of old blank paper Franklin held in front of his face. Franklin removed his biofocals from his brest pocket and handed them to Hewson.

"Read," he commanded.

Further confused, Hewson put on the bifocals. The paper is blank—was he missing something? Hewson struggled to contain his mounting anxiety but he felt the eyes of the congregation piercing through him, studying his soul, judging his weakness. He was certain they were somehow aware of every shortcoming, every shameful failure. Hewson looked to Darwin, who was staring back, waiting for him to read the contents of the page. He looked to Franklin, then the congregation of tall candles and hot eyes. Hewson was begining to sweat.

"Do not panic," said Darwin. "There is hope for your vision to improve."

Franklin removed the biofocals from Hewson's face, folded them and placed them inside of his breast pocket.

Darwin continued. "The Master orders preparation for the surgery to commence," he said.

Franklin selected the small cloth rag from the tray of surgical tools and wiped Hewson's eyes with it. All of it happened so fast. Hewson shuddered as Franklin picked up the long tweezers. Franklin bent over and looked Hewson dead in the eyes.

"Proceed," said Darwin.

In unison, the men raised their candles above their heads. Despite his efforts to remain calm, Hewson's breath quickened and his chest heaved as the metal tool came toward his face. He shut his eye, then felt a sting. Franklin plucked a single eyebrow hair, then another, and another.

"These are symbolic actions," Franklin said. "None of which are without meaning."

Relieved, Hewson almost let out a chuckle as Franklin placed the tweezers among the other surgical tools on the tray.

"The Candidate places his hand on the Master's amulet," said Darwin.

Franklin removed the eye of providence from around his neck and held the amulet in his open palm. Hewson placed his right hand over it, as if swearing an oath on the Bible. Darwin handed Franklin another piece of old paper, which Franklin then held in front of Hewson's face.

"Try reading again," he said.

The page was filled with the most skillful handwritten calligraphy Hewson had ever seen.

"I, William Hewson, of my own free will and accord, do hereby most solemnly and sincerely promise and swear, that I will hail, ever conceal, and never reveal any of the secrets, arts, parts, point or points, of the Master's Degree, to any person or persons whomsoever, except that it be a true and lawful brother of this Degree."

The watchful eyes of the congregation gazed at Hewson from behind their candles as he read, like one giant, unified animal, throbbing like flames, hanging on every word.

"I will acknowledge and obey all due signs and summons sent to me from my Master. Further, I will keep a worthy brother's secrets inviolable, when communicated to and received by me as such. All this I most solemnly, sincerely promise and swear, with a firm and steady resolution to perform the same, without any hesitation, under no less penalty that that of having my body severed in two, my bowels taken from thence and burned to ashes, the ashes scattered before the four winds of heaven, that no more remembrance might be had of so vile and wicked a wretch as I would be, should I ever, knowingly, violate this my Master's obligation."

For a moment, Hewson met Franklin's hard stare glaring back at him. It made him swallow hard.

"So help me God, and keep me steadfast in the due performance of the same," Hewson concluded.

Next, Darwin spoke with an air of great authority.

"This stroke is the sign, the symbol, and the beginning of the confidentiality and familiarity that the brother, from now on companion, can expect of us," he boomed.

The congregation of men, their faces illuminated by candle flame like distorted hallucinations, spoke in unison.

"Congratulations, Brother. Now you can see."

The Initiate looked to his Master as he clipped the amulet around his protégé's neck.

"Congratulations, Job. Now you can see," said Darwin. "Judas, your Master, will show you to your seat."

Franklin led Hewson back to their seats.

Darwin continued. "As the play begins, our hero, Mankind…"

Darwin pointed to one of the seated men in the front row, who was wearing a grotesque mask with an elongated nose that drooped down past a sharp, demonic chin. The face sent a chill through William Hewson–it had dark, deep holes for eyes.

Darwin proceeded, "…ignores the council of his Good Angel and allows his Bad Angel to lead him into the service of World."

Another actor in a blue mask with thin slits for eyes, nose, and mouth, sprang to his feet.

Darwin went on, "Lust and Folly seduce Mankind and dress the hero in expensive clothes…"

Two young boys dressed as Roman Nymphs wearing togas and laurel wreaths appeared from nowhere and took the stage, and seduced Mankind. They danced around him, rubbing themselves against his body.

Hewson looked to Franklin, who returned his protege's gaze out of the corner of his eye, along with that wry, Franklin smile.

Mankind, now missing his toga, stood before the congregation totally naked except for that horrible mask and an artificial red phallus worn over his penis. The phallus was attached to a string wrapped around his neck, which kept it erect. The boys wrapped a golden tunic around his body and attached it with a large brown leather belt with a massive silver buckle, bejeweled with diamonds and rubies.

"…and lead him to the scaffold of coveteousness…"

The nymphs led Mankind to the other side of the stage where World stood waiting.

"…where mankind accepts the Seven Deadly Sins. All is not lost, though, for Shrift and Penance appear…"

The actors playing Shrift and Penance jumped in out of the darkness wearing bright green leotards and harlequin masks, each grabbing hold of Mankind's hands.

"…they convince Mankind to repent and place him in the Castle of Perseverance where he will be protected from sin by Seven Moral Virutes."

Franklin gave Hewson a slight, wise nod.

"Mankind's enemies, World, Flesh, and The Devil…"

Hewson could have sworn he saw the actors Flesh and The Devil materialize out of thin air, for he could not image from where they would have come. Suddenly, two men in hideous demonic masks stood on either side of the actor playing World.

"…attack the Castle of Perseverance but are repulsed by the Virtues armed with roses."

The three devils swirled around Mankind, who crossed both hands over his chest, then held them up, palms out, with both thumbs crossed over his palms. The devils swirl away into the darkness as mysteriously as they appeared. Hewson's blood ran cold—it really did seem as if supernatural events were playing out before his very eyes, as if in a horrible dream, but this was no dream. Indeed, this goulish event was taking place in order to commemorate him and this new family of important, influential men he had sworn his life to. He swallowed hard, but his mouth was bone dry.

"Next, Covetousness tempts Mankind with an offer of wealth and peace of mind. If only he will give up his sacred Knowledge."

The actor playing Covetousness wore a long white robe and held a porcelain mask on a stick over his face. The mask wore a grotesque, greedy smile. Covetousness approached Mankind with his free hand outstretched.

"Mankind thinks about accepting but is struck down by Death, illustrating that mortality may collect its toll at any moment."

Like the others, Covetousness dissolved into the darkness. In his place stood Death, wearing a long black robe and holding a porcelain skull mask over his face. Death threw his robe over Mankind and they both vanished into thin air. There was no applause. Hewson wondered if he were still sane. Had he been given some kind of mind-altering drug or did this occult ceremony really have the power to materialze strange entities? There was no way. Surely, some trick of the eye was responsible for what he had seen.

Again, Darwin addressed the congregation of seated men. "On the Second Degree Of Fellowcraft, the Philosopher, David Hume." Then, the master of ceremonies took to his seat, a towering black velvet umbrella dome. David Hume took his place before the congregation, speaking in Latin.

"Descartes said, "I suppose the body to be nothing but a statue or machine made of earth,"" said Hume as he placed his fingers to the center of his forehead.

"Descartes believed the pineal body to be full of "animal spirits" which he described as "a very fine wind, or a very lively and pure flame.""

The stoic congregation gave their undivided attention.

"Indeed, there is a distinction between the human being and the human person. The human being is a mechanical sack of meat. The human person is this *fine wind*, this *very lively* and *pure flame* that can be extinguished while the body goes on living. Bodies without Souls."

Franklin looked to Hewson, his eyes burning with white-hot intensity.

CHAPTER 14

THE MARRIAGE

DOWN IN THE cellar, Franklin and Hewson stood over the hollowed-out corpse of the criminal lying outstretched, holding handkerchiefs to their faces while flies swarmed around the ripening body. In the corner of the cellar stood the stone box covered by a large slab. Hewson removed the slab and was hit in the face with an unbearable stench. He vomited at the sight of a rotting corpse with a slit throat lying on top of other rotting bodies. When the Initiate turned to his Master he was met with piercing, fiery eyes glaring back at him over the handkerchief covering his nose and mouth. Hewson took a moment to collect himself, then picked up the mostly-hollow corpse from the operating table and dumped it in the box on top of the other rotting bodies.

That night, an oil lamp burned on Franklin's desk illuminating several jars containing floating pineal glands. The old polymath wrote in his thick leather-bound journal, occasionally dipping his white feather quill in a brass inkwell. On the page these words were inscribed:

VARIANCE IN QUALITY OF THE HUMAN SOUL

Beneath this, Franklin drew diagrams of pineal glands with captions explaining the conditions of the subjects from which they were extracted. He had given Hewson a pair of his patented bifocals to assist his vision while working on his manuscript. The invention helped his sight greatly. Now in his office, Hewson wrote in his journal beside a blood-splattered page of crude, hasty drawings made during the earlier dissection.

A NEW STUDY OF THE RED AND WHITE BLOOD CELLS

A corked vial of blood sat on his desk beside a small microscope made of brass, wood, and glass. Hewson uncorked the vial of blood and, using a small dropper, sucked up a sample and placed a drop on the glass slide, then looked through the viewfinder. What he saw was truly astonishing—microscopic blood cells danced about then joined together to form an image of the "Eye Of Providence," that cryptic eye within a triangle on Franklin's amulet and Dr. Lambert's ring. Hewson whipped his head back and rubbed his black, tired eyes. Was he losing his mind? Then suddenly, a revelation. He wrote in his journal:

BLOOD COAGULATION – A NEW THEORY

Polly entered the room but Hewson continued writing without so much as a nod to acknowledge her presence. Lightning had struck—a gift from above. He was sailing the crest of a brand new wave.

"Have you been so hard at work you have forgotten me?" she queried.

"Not at all, my love," Hewson replied. "I miss you terribly but the world needs to know the true shape of red blood cells. They are flat, not round."

The lovers shared a laugh. Polly sat down on Hewson's lap and their laughter turned into a giddy, passionate kiss. She stood and grabbed him by the hands.

"Your blood cells can wait, but mine cannot," she said.

Polly led Hewson to the bed where they collapsed, entwined. "You will pay attention to me now," she said and they continued kissing, undressing, and slipping into gentle lovemaking.

In Parliament, Lord Fredrick North presided over the Council Of Lords, like a fat, shiny-faced sea bass. The diagonal slant of his forehead extended to the very top of his head, well beyond the conventional limits of a hairline. His hair was white and culminated in a tight oval at its zenith, the sides of which were curled just above his ears like a couple of cannoli.

The Council Of Lords—what a collection of characters. Some wore massive, curly wigs, some sported tight little buns and curly-cues above their ears. They sat under a massive half-dome ceiling surrounded by high, turquoise walls trimmed in gold-gilt. Lord North flapped his glistening lips in mid-dissertation.

"...the discussion regarding the unrest in the American Colonies over the Hutchinson Letters, which contained sensitive information from the Crown in private correspondence between two royal officials. These letters were somehow leaked to the Boston press and printed. The incident incited riots in the Colonies. Now, rumours are circulating that the Colonists plan to demand freedom from the Crown of Mother England and are willing to use force to become a sovereign nation. There has been an unresolved duel here in London over the matter with another scheduled to settle the issue once and for all."

Solicitor General Lord Wedderburn stood amongst the crowd of Parliamentary members seated below. As usual, he was dressed to the hilt in a bright red velvet cape that covered most of his body, clasped around his neck by a diamond-studded gold broach, his long white hair wavy past his shoulders. His face was almost as red as his coat.

"Whoever is guilty of this treasonous act will duly pay!" he shouted.

Franklin was noticeably absent from that day's proceedings. Murmurings abounded amoungst the gossipy lords. In lieu of attending his usual duty, the revolutionary was in his office at 36 Craven Street, writing a letter with a long white feather quill, his bifocals resting on the tip of his nose. He folded the letter, dripped red candle wax on the fold, and secured a piece of his future legacy with the stamp of his seal, B.F.

Later, in the Craven Street Gallery, the great French painter Joseph Duplessis stood before a large easel rubbing paint on the canvas with his brush. He looked up for a moment to have another look at his subject. Dr. Benjamin Franklin sat still, stoic, staring straight ahead. The Frenchman spoke with a heavy accent while he worked.

"My father was a talented painter, but he was a surgeon by trade," he said. "He was also a Mason."

"Ah, good man," Franklin replied, speaking through tight lips and trying not to move too much. "You succeeded in making a career out of your father's passion."

"Yes, he taught me to paint but he did not support my wanting to make a career as an artist. He thought I would starve. He wanted me to be a surgeon. He told me that as an artist there is no security," said Duplessis, dabbing away at his canvas.

"Security without Liberty is called Prison," Franklin replied.

After several days of sitting for hours at a time, Franklin's iconic portrait was almost finished. On the canvas, Duplessis' brush delicately stroked the sides of Franklin's mouth into a mysterious, Mona Lisa smile.

At dinner, knives sliced into pheasants on silver platters along the candlelit table. Franklin ate his veggies. King kept the wine flowing as the diners conversed and drank. The Widow Mrs. Stevenson downed another glass and King refilled it.

"How are your studies coming along, gentleman?" she slurred.

"Very fine, indeed," said Franklin. "Our boy William has almost mapped the entire lymphatic system."

Hewson gave a polite nod. The Widow's drinking made him uncomfortable.

"I, for one, am chiefly concerned with locating the human soul," Franklin continued.

Franklin, Polly, and The Widow gave a heady laugh. Hewson caught on and forced a polite laugh, too.

"Next we shall begin working on live bodies!" Franklin said and they all laughed harder.

Mima the hunchbacked slave hobbled over to the glass armonica. She sent it spinning with a single crank, dipped her knobby, arthritic fingers in the glass bowl of water, and set them against the crystal, playing shrill, dissonant tones. The diners fell silent.

"Not tonight Mima," said Franklin. "Not tonight."

She shut off the armonica without a word and hobbled away in silence.

In the smoking-room after dinner, Franklin and Hewson sat in tall velvet chairs enjoying their long pipes by the fire.

"The ignorance of others is not my moral responsibility," Franklin said. "But never lie. Honesty is the best policy."

The blood had fallen from Hewson's face. He was pale and felt clammy.

"You are out of sorts," said Franklin.

"I do not think it is morally sound to operate on live bodies," Hewson managed. "What happens when we are finished?"

"We kill them," Franklin said. "Throw them in the box."

"Dr. Franklin…"

"Remember what Descartes said," Franklin interrupted. "I

suppose the body to be nothing but a statue or machine made of earth. Down on Gin Lane there are plenty of living bodies missing that *very lively* and *pure flame.*"

Franklin could tell that Hewson was far from convinced. He pressed on.

"How can one claim to know how blood moves through the body without first seeing how it is done? For the purpose of our studies, it is perfectly all right to kill living beings that are simply *being*—that serve no purpose and are therefore parasitic to men. Insects, certain animals, Indians, drunks, and so on, for the purpose of increasing understanding and forging new pathways. If we do not do it someone else will, and it will be their names that history will remember."

Hewson could see his Master was not giving in. He made a compelling argument.

"Besides," Franklin continued. "'Tis' impossible to satiate the curiosity of the Natural Philosopher. It is simply the next logical step. We must acquire a live one to operate on next."

This made Hewson swallow hard. He knew it was true.

That night, Polly found Hewson walled-off and cagey.

"What is wrong?" she asked.

"Nothing," he said. Polly gave him a look that suggested she was far from satisfied with this answer.

"It is just…Dr. Franklin and his colleagues…"

"Relax, love," Polly said. "You are doing fine. Dr. Franklin has the utmost faith in you."

"I am afraid you do not quite understand," Hewson tried to explain.

"William," said Polly. "I think I am pregnant."

In a sunny, serene park, surrounded by jasmine and roses, Franklin gave the beautiful bride away to his protégé. As Franklin joined Polly's hands with those of her beloved he stared into Hewson's eyeballs with white-hot intensity. Erasmus Darwin, the officiator of the wedding, received the couple and began his sermon as Mima played "Water Music" by Handel on the glass armonica.

"Ladies and Gentleman," Darwin announced. "We are gathered here today to witness the sacred union of two souls—William and Polly."

The bride smiled at her groom, the groom smiled at his bride, and Franklin watched over the proceedings with his white-hot gaze. Then, total darkness. The flame of a single burning candle illuminated the faces of Franklin and Hewson in profile, together in a dark room. The flame burned between their faces.

"The definition of *sin* is an act that separates a man from his Creator, and is, therefore, subjective," Franklin said. "Consider this—what if an act that separates one man from his Creator unites another man with his?"

From the deep past, The *London Hope* clipper ship sailed the stormy seas. Young Ben was in the death room with the bloated corpse of the woman who collapsed in the bunks and died of a stroke. Ben had his knickers down around his knees. He spat on his dick to get it wet and shoved it in her corpse and fucked it until he came.

In another dark, candlelit room, a group of men shrouded in hooded capes stood around a bed of nails where lay the naked body of William Hewson wearing only the Eye of Providence amulet around his neck. The room was littered with occult and Masonic objects. Although the men standing at Hewson's feet wore hoods, enough of their faces could be seen to tell it was Erasmus Darwin and Lord North, who presided over the House Of Lords. Lord North addressed his understudy.

"Lazarus," he said to Erasmus Darwin. "Attend to your protégé."

"Judas," Darwin said to Franklin. "Attend to your protégé."

Franklin stood at the head of the bed of nails wearing a sword sheathed in a holster. He unsheathed his sword and pressed the tip to Hewson's forehead. Lord North, Erasmus Darwin, and Ben Franklin spoke in unison.

"Job," they said. "This is the top of the deepest level, the depths of which are infinite."

Hewson stared straight up, trying not to tremble. The rest of the cloaked figures unsheathed their swords and pressed them to Hewson's naked body.

"Brother Job," said Lord North. "We hold the key to the secrets of the world. There are many secrets among us, however, we keep no secrets between us."

Hewson finched, then began to tremble.

"Tell us your worst, and we shall give you our best," Lord North said.

Hewson's trembling escaped his control. He was as shaky as a cup of pudding. The cloaked figures pressed their swords a little harder into his flesh but still not hard enough to break the skin.

"I sodomized another man!" he shouted.

Against a Masonic altar filled with dripping candles, William Hewson, wearing only a goat's head and the Eye Of Providence around his neck, sodomized another man, who also wore a goat's head. The hooded faces of Lord North, Erasmus Darwin, David Hume, Ben Franklin, and a mysterious Fat Man wearing a monocle, watched closely. As Hewson reached climax he was struck by a powerful vision—an image of the Path to the Sun flashed rhythmically in his mind's eye. He saw himself and Franklin standing on a black and white checkerboard tile platform floating in the cosmos. Roman columns flanked a winding white marble path that disappeared into a desert horizon at the end of which burned a massive Sun with a black dot in the middle. Franklin and Hewson met at a set of three marble steps that led to the Pathway to the Sun. Together, the two ascended the steps to the Path.

CHAPTER 15

ANOTHER LIVE ONE

FOUR YEARS PASSED in rapid succession. Hewson and Franklin operated on many Gin Lane subjects, each man getting closer to his goal. For Hewson, it was understanding the blood. He had almost mapped the entire lymphatic system and made strides in documenting the molecular structure of blood cells, as well as major discoveries regarding the fibrin coagulation process of healing. Franklin was determined to map the soul, which he was well on his way to doing, informed by Descartes' theories, ancient occult wisdom traditions, and Pythagorean geometry..

Presently, Hewson was on a much needed holiday with his young family, at his wife's insistence. He and Polly sat on a blanket in the grass enjoying a picnic watching their twin children at play, a boy and a girl both four years of age.

"Look at our life together," said Polly.

"I know," replied Hewson. "It seems too good to be true."

He took the last sip of wine from his cup and Polly poured him another.

"You were right," he said. "We must take to the countryside every now and again. All of the mounting pressure back in London…"

"William, stop," Polly ordered. "Allow yourself a moment of enjoyment."

Hewson chuckled to himself. "You are right again," he said. "I have been so consumed by my work I can hardly see the good that is right before my eyes."

The lovers shared a soft kiss. Their children were at play in the grass, sword fighting with sticks.

"I am King Arthur and you are Lancelot," shouted their little girl between stick jabs with her twin brother.

"No, I am King Arthur and you are Lancelot!" he shouted back at her.

Their names were Elizabeth and Thomas, twins both aged four years. In fact, they were almost the same age as Hewson when his twin sister died and revealed to him his life's purpose. They were everything to Hewson—cherubs from heaven—especially his little girl.

"No, I am King Arthur and you are a dragon and I must slay you!" Elizabeth shouted as she pretended to stab Thomas with her stick sword. Her brother went down, playing along. Hewson and Polly laughed at the sight of this. Their children ran to them and sat on their father's lap.

"Father, what happens after we die?" Elizabeth asked.

"That is a big question, my love," he said.

"How come?" asked Thomas.

"Well, no one really knows," replied Hewson. "Where were you before you were born?"

A smile stretched over his young daughter's face as she wondered about this.

"I do not know!" she shouted, then fell over laughing while her father tickled her.

That night, William and Polly lay together in bed having just finished making love.

"Where do you see our lives in five years?" Polly asked.

"We will be living in our own home with another child," replied Hewson.

The lovers smiled and kissed. "By then I will have finished my thesis on the lympathic system, which will be recognized by the Royal Society."

Polly rolled her eyes and they shared a giddy laugh.

"Ah yes," she said. "William Hewson, the great blood surgeon."

"I just want to give people a chance that my sister never had."

"You are a great surgeon, William. A great husband, and a great father."

Sick patients in wooden-framed beds lined the walls of the large open rooms at The Royal Infirmary. Dr. William Hewson was now the head surgeon, thanks to his connections with Franklin's London colleagues. A nurse in a light dress and bonnet tended to a cauldron hanging over a hearth fire at the front of the room, which was filled with ambient coughing and wheezing coming from the beds. Other nurses walked from bed to bed, checking up on their patients, and preparing some of them for bloodletting. Dr. Hewson stood at the bed of a feverish patient, a middle aged man with a strange bulge on one side of his neck lying shirtless under his sweat-soaked bedsheet.

"Good afternoon, Mr..."

"Gordon," the man said in a strained, raspy voice.

"Mr. Gordon. Very good. We are going to remove that growth in your neck today."

"Oh goody," said Gordon.

One of the nurses placed a large wooden bowl at the sick man's bedside.

"I must warn you," Hewson said. "This is not going to be a comfortable surgery."

"I figured as much," the patient rasped.

"Yes, but your survival depends on it. We must remove that growth," said the good doctor.

"Hop to it then," said Gordon.

The nurse handed Gordon a bottle of gin. The patient steadied himself, then began chugging the firewater. Dr. Hewson unrolled a cloth of surgical tools on a table at the other side of the bed. Though Gordon gagged occasionally, he managed to down the entire bottle to the last drop.

"Chop, chop," he said.

The nurse placed a cork in Gordon's mouth. He bit down on it hard, grunting up his courage as Hewson placed a scalpel blade to the heaving bulge in his neck. Gordon's bloody screams could be heard from the hallway.

Hewson remembered this moment as he stood at his daughter's bedside, her brow wet with fever sweat, a bulge forming at one side of her neck perceptible only to the touch of a doctor who had encountered one before.

"She seems to have the fever only when she sleeps, yet she is not hot to the touch," he said to Polly.

"She has not been right in weeks. What are we to do?"

"I do not know yet," Hewson said. "But I am going to find out."

That night after dinner, Franklin and Hewson sat fireside smoking their pipes.

"Tonight is the night, my boy," Franklin said. "Are you ready?"

Hewson nodded, but he was far from ready.

Franklin and Hewson walked London's foggy cobblestone streets by the glowing light of the moon after midnight. Inside of a Gin Lane dram shop, a red-nosed tramp ordered another shot from a barmaid skeleton wearing a petticoat. The skeleton held an expressionless porcelain mask of a female face in front of its skull with one hand and poured a shot of gin with the other. The red-nosed tramp downed the shot, then heaved, but managed not to spew. He set the glass down on the bar, walked out into the foggy streets and stumbled into the gutter, where he passed out. Not long after, Franklin and Hewson came upon the streets of Gin Lane, where they spotted the lifeless tramp, passed out cold, his dirty, ripped smock covered in vomit. Franklin kicked the bottom of the tramp's foot. Nothing. With urgency, Franklin kicked at the tramp's foot until he began to regain consciousness, the men standing over him coming into hazy focus.

"Hello, councilor!" slurred the tramp.

"Hello, old chap," Franklin replied. "What do you say we have a drink?"

The tramp took ahold of Hewson's outstretched hand, and after a time, got to his feet. The anatomists walked the stumbling tramp to the alley behind 36 Craven Street, through the gate, to the flower bed of rose bushes. The tramp was in and out of consciousness, leaning heavily on Hewson. Franklin opened the cellar trap door, lit his oil lantern, and led the way down to the cellar, followed by Hewson and the stumbling tramp. In the candlelit basement, Franklin handed the tramp a fifth of gin. The tramp downed the bottle in a fury, heaving between chugs. It was absolute poison—pure fire—but the tramp could not get enough. The men watched until he dropped to the floor with a thud and the clinking bottle. Hewson cut away the tramp's vomit-soaked clothes, then spread his naked body over the operating table. Franklin felt the tramp's neck—the pulse was barely there. Hewson unrolled his cloth of scalpels on the table. Franklin had daggers in his eyes—he shot them at Hewson. He had been insisting they operate on live bodies for the past four years and now the time had finally come. He knew Hewson's position on the matter well. Would he have the mettle to pass this test? Franklin wondered. Sensing the pressure, the surgeon summoned his courage and picked up a knife. He steadied himself, turned off his mind, then sliced into the unconscious tramp's breathing chest.

"Well done is better than well said," said Franklin.

The polymath picked up his trepanning device, stuck it to the tramp's forehead, and drilled with vigor. Hewson, sweaty-browed and wide-eyed, reached into the tramp's open chest toward the beating heart, admiring the majesty of witnessing first-hand the mechanics of the blood pumping through a living human body. Franklin was in mid-drill when the tramp's eyes opened followed by a deafening screech.

A lantern lit in the second story window. Hearing the distant screams, a terror-stricken Polly scrambled into the Widow Mrs. Stevenson's room and slammed her lantern down on her bedisde table. In desperation, she slapped her mother's face several times in succession, trying to wake the drunken widow. Having no success, and now in a manic state, Polly flung herself to the floor, crying and writhing in terror.

Down in the cellar, Franklin and Hewson attempted to quiet the tramp by pouring more gin down his screaming throat but the tramp vomited the firewater into his open chest, prompting him to cry out louder, the trepanning drill still lodged in his forehead. Franklin grabbed a hold of the drill and forced a last few cranks. He ripped it out of the tramp's head, dug his forefinger inside the hole, extracted the pineal gland, and dropped it inside of an open mason jar full of clear liquid. The brutality of the moment sent Hewson into shock. He stood there watching with vacant eyes as Franklin picked up a brick from the floor and smashed the tramp's face to mushy pulp. Finally, he was dead. Franklin screwed the lid on the jar and set it on the shelf beside the others. Hewson removed the stone slab from the box and threw the tramp's wasted body inside, impervious to the stench emanating from the hole.

Hewson was ruined. Franklin was able to convince Polly that

the screaming she heard must have been in a dream, or possibly, a distant pack of wolves having scored a fresh kill. Being the night of a full moon, the men had an alibi. They were at the Soho House of Erasmus Darwin, as they were every full moon.

Hewson's conscience was plagued by a recurring nightmare. He lay naked on the operating table, the bloodied and disfigured tramp, also naked, chest wide open, guts hanging out, a gaping hole in his forehead, standing over him. The tramp stuffed a bottle of gin into Hewson's mouth, breaking his teeth, emptying the firewater into his gagging face. Next, he watched as the tramp flayed his chest open with his own knife, and dug out his guts, passing them to King the Slave, who helped empty him out into a wooden bucket on the floor.

Hewson sat upright in bed, screaming. Polly, terrified by his blood-curdling screams, shook him awake. As he came to, the panicked look on Polly's face frightened him even more, causing him to scream louder, then spring out of bed, drenched in terror sweat. He collapsed into Polly's arms, both sobbing uncontrollably.

"I cannot go on like this," Hewson confessed. "Franklin is mad!"

Polly's countenance shifted to anger as she processed what was said.

"All you care about is your work with Dr. Franklin! All you have ever been concerned with is your career—our daughter is sick, you bastard!"

Hewson found himself alone in hell.

CHAPTER 16

THE TRIAL OF JOB

FRANKLIN AND POLLY, each with a pair of metal scissors and their sleeves rolled up, were at work in the rose garden, pruning the rosebushes in the flowerbed above the cellar trap door. Polly, wearing a light dress and bonnet, placed her scissors around an old thorny twig. Franklin stopped her before she could make the cut.

"Always prune away from the outward-facing rosebud," he said.

To demonstrate, Franklin clipped a sprig of dead leaves away from an outward-facing rosebud. Polly found her own sprig of withered leaves beside an outward-facing rosebud and cut it off.

"Polly, I have been meaning to discuss something with you but I do not want to upset you," Franklin said.

"It's William, isn't it?" she said. "That damned manuscript."

Franklin hesitated. "I think the pressure he is under might be damaging his health."

They continued trimming to stave off the awkward silence that followed. After a time, Franklin pressed the issue.

"How are things between the two of you lately?" he queried.

"Not good," Polly said. "He hardly sleeps."

"He must go somewhere and rest awhile," said Franklin.

"Our little Elizabeth is sick, I cannot be without William now," Polly protested.

"Mima will continue to care for Dorothy," Franklin assured.

"Presently, I feel that William is the sicker one,' he continued. "I will spare you the gritty details as to why but frankly, I fear for his sanity. He must have a few weeks' rest."

Franklin cut out a dead thorny branch from the side of the bush and tossed it away.

At the Royal Infirmary, Gordon lay asleep in bed with a bloody cloth tourniquet tied around his neck. The nurse came to his bedside with a bowl of water and set it on the end table. She leaned over him and carefully removed the tourniquet. Dr. Hewson stood at the foot of the bed watching the nurse work as Gordon gradually awakened with a groan. A large stitched-up gash ran along the side of his neck.

"Good morning, Mr. Gordon," said Dr. Hewson. "Good news, I was able to remove the entire growth. Once the pain subsides I am sure you will find a swift return to health."

Gordon, too weak to speak, raised his hand to acknowledge the news.

Later that night, Hewson stayed up late, as he did every night, at work in his office on his manuscript. He had deep, dark bags under his sleepless, bloodshot eyes. He dipped his feather quill in the inkwell and wrote in his journal:

BLOOD CELLS AND THE IMMUNE SYSTEM

Downstairs, Mima brought a bowl of hot soup to Elizabeth's bedside. The child was now very weak and did not have much of an appetite.

"Sit up child," Mima said. "This here soup will soothe your aching throat."

Dorothy managed to sit up and take a couple of spoonfuls before slinking down again.

Franklin was up late as well, sitting in his velvet chair smoking a pipe by the fire. Hewson, thin, pale, and disheveled, approached Franklin and sat in the chair across from him like he had done so many nights after dinner. Franklin eyed him with a tinge of disdain.

"Do not crack on me now boy," Franklin said, puffing on his pipe.

"I do not think I can continue," said the rail-thin, hollow-eyed Hewson.

"When you are finished changing, you're finished," Franklin tossed back.

"I don't like what I am becoming," Hewson replied.

"You don't know that," said Franklin. "You haven't become it yet."

Hewson took this in. Then, Franklin pounced.

"Are you really prepared to throw away your life's work because you are worried about exchanging a wasted souse for the greatest scientific achievements that will benefit all of mankind?"

Hewson had nothing to say. His bones were tired.

Franklin continued, saying, "History remembers men who write stories worth reading. Don't give up just as your's is taking shape. You can do anything you set your mind to."

"I am on the verge of a breakthrough," Hewson said. "But I do not think I can go on."

"The souls of criminals and drunkards are of poor quality. These men are irredeemable," Franklin said. "Therefore, there is no moral problem with using an arfarfan'arf for experimentation. Our surgeries are advancing science for the good of all."

Exhausted and broken, Hewson feigned satisfaction with Franklin's assessment of their methods but he lacked the strength to keep his thoughts inside. The dam in his mind had sprung a leak. Fissures in stone cracked and burst and his thoughts flowed out.

"I feel as though I have been cursed," he said, looking at the ground. "I cannot live with myself but I cannot live without my work."

Franklin listened, a thoughtful mentor in Hewson's time of need. Feeling a bit of safety in this new territory, his protege continued—he needed answers.

"Why am I called Job?" Hewson asked.

"My dear boy," Franklin chuckled. "Under the watchful eye, we are all given a biblical name that conceals our ultimate purpose and determines our future within the Brotherhood. We were all selected for a reason—even I was selected. Can you imagine how I felt when I was given the name, Judas?" he said, chuckling again to himself.

Hewson hung on every word.

"As a young apprentice," continued Franklin, "I did not know my destiny but I have learned it, piece by piece, through years of service in the Brotherhood. Slowly, my purpose was revealed to me. I would have been crushed under the full weight of this knowledge had it been given to me whole, all at once, right away. Luckily, this was not the case. As the Path unfolds I simply chose to always take the next right action and I have been led to a place of great Power and Prestige."

Hewson could see where this was going. Although he half-expected such an answer, he drank in Franklin's generous response. Somehow, it helped quench his thirst. He had been so alone with this suffering, so empty and dry.

"If I continue, which I will," Franklin said, "my experience thus far has convinced me that the Annuls of History will look Favorably upon the Legacy of this fat old fool long after he is gone. We protect our Brother's Legacies as strictly as we protect our Sacred Knowledge. Be patient. Sometimes you have to go through the worst to get to the best."

Hewson could not simply *be patient*. He was complicit in the murder of innocent people, and unlike his Master, had yet to experience the full benefit of this work.

"Well then, Master," he said. "What is to be my legacy? What is my purpose in all of this?"

"Even I do not know that yet," Franklin said. "You will have to keep going to find out. However, all of the clues you need right now are in the name. Do you know the story of Job?"

Whatever strange comfort Hewson had gleaned from Franklin's previous answer had gone away. Now, he was getting irritated.

"Yes, I do," he said. "God strikes a perfectly fine man down with all of life's miseries and misfortunes for some childish test of allegiance but still the fool won't turn his back on his tormentor. It is a pitiful story. A comfort for poor religious simpletons to feel better about their shit lot in life."

Franklin was amused by Hewson's assessment of the Book of Job.

"Not quite," he said. "You have parts of it but not the whole story. The story of Job goes like this. One day, Satan went to God and told him that Man is inherently wicked. God counters this claim with Job, a truly exemplary young man—he possessed a certain amount of material wealth, had a nice family, and the respect of his countrymen. Job was upright and blameless and on top of all that," Franklin said with raised eyebrows, "he was extremely devoted to God. But Satan tells God that Job is only devoted to him because God has blessed him with a wonderful life. Satan requests God's permission to test Job's loyalty. God permits Satan to do his worst in tormenting Job to test this claim. So, Satan robs Job of everything— kills his family, takes away his wealth and good standing. Still, Job keeps his faith in God but Satan raises another point—Job still has his health. Men can endure anything so long as they are healthy. Job's health is his wealth. So God permits Satan to take that away, too. Soon, Job is cursed with painful, oozing, infected boils, covering his body from head to foot. Still, Job does not turn his back on God. Instead, he turns inward to search himself for ways in which he can improve and become more perfect in the eyes of his Master."

Hewson listened closely. Franklin let that sink in for a moment, then continued.

"Having endured Satan's tribulations, God rewarded Job for his loyalty with a renewed family, twice as much wealth as he had before, and blessed him with a long, healthy, and contented life. Job finally died at the ripe old age of one hundred and forty, with generations of grandchildren and plenty of fruitful years behind him…and we still speak his name today."

Hewson was coming to a place of acceptance. He knew there was no changing his Master's mind.

"I see," he said.

"Come on," said Franklin. "Let's go out and get ourselves another live one."

After midnight, Franklin and Hewson hit the foggy London streets on another trip down to Gin Lane. This time, however, they were being followed. Unbeknownst to them, a mysterious hooded figure traced their every step. Before they even hit Gin Lane, a wandering drunk in a ratty tricorn hat and ripped frock stumbled toward them.

"This blunderbuss," said Franklin.

The anatomists flanked the drunk, walking alongside him, his arms slung over their shoulders. They walked him all the way back to the alley behind 36 Craven Street and the mysterious hooded figure followed the whole time, watching from the gate as Franklin opened the trap door beside the flowerbed and descended into the earth, followed by Hewson and their drunk.

The surgery was a bad struggle. Hewson stood with one arm crossed over his midsection, chest heaving, catching his breath. The drunk lay naked on the operating table, chest and ribcage wide open, a gaping hole in his forehead, barely breathing.

"It's all one system," said Hewson, looking a million miles away to nowhere. He had seen the lymphatic system at work in a living body, regardless of whether or not it carried a "quality" soul. His theories had been confirmed.

"The lymphatic and immune systems are one system." he repeated to himself.

Franklin patted him on the back then threw his arm around the surgeon. His boy made a hard-won breakthrough. Hewson removed the stone slab and tossed the drunk inside the box, atop a mounting pile of rotting bodies. He was no longer affected by the stench. The drunk was still breathing a little bit as Hewson closed the slab.

Back in his office that night, after cleaning himself up with a cold sponge bath, Hewson wrote in his journal by the light of an oil lamp.

THE IMMUNE SYSTEM – NEW FINDINGS

In the smoking room, Franklin sat in his velvet chair smoking his long pipe beside the roaring fire when Hewson entered, holding a thick leatherbound manuscript.

"It is finished," he said.

"Well, bring it here," said Franklin. "Let's see it."

Hewson handed the book to Franklin. He opened it to the first page. In artfully arranged print, it read:

BLOOD CELLS AND THE IMMUNE SYSTEM, BY Dr. WILLIAM HEWSON

Franklin closed the manuscript, leaned into the fireplace, and held it over the flames.

"Surely you will offer a dedication of this work to your Master, will you not, Job?"

"Why yes, of course!" Hewson shouted, flames lapping at the past five years of his life. Franklin slowly removed the manuscript from the fire, unharmed.

"William Hewson," he said. "The Father Of Hematology. The Royal Society will be pleased to count you among its membership."

CHAPTER 17

THE INDUCTION

PORTRAITS OF GREAT men in gold-gilt frames lined the tall, deep-green walls of The London Royal Society For Improving Natural Knowledge. The hall was filled with dignitaries, nobles, and natural philosophers, all dressed in their finest clothes. They had gathered to witness the induction of Dr. William Hewson to the Royal Society and his receipt of the Copley Medal for his advancements in the study of the blood. He would now be counted among the likes of Sir Isaac Newton. William Hewson—the father of hematology.

Earl Macclesfield, the president of the Royal Society, stood at the front of the stage holding the society's highest honor in his hand.

"The Copely Medal Award for advancements in the study of the blood, Dr. William Hewson," he shouted from the top of his lungs.

The hall was filled with applause from the distinguished crowd as Hewson took to the front of the stage and received his award. Darwin and Franklin sat side by side, applauding as Earl Maccelsfield placed the Copely Medal around Hewson's neck.

"Give the boy a break," Darwin said. "Let him enjoy his new-found fame a little while."

In Parliament, another kind of ceremony was taking place. Lord North presided over the House Of Lords—he was almost through reading a confession letter to the stunned congregation.

"With great and sincere esteem, your most humble servant, Dr. Benjamin Franklin," he finished.

Solicitor General Lord Wedderburn stood, his hair swinging like the long ears of an outraged hound.

"Treason!" he shouted.

All of the other Lords erupted in discussion. Lord North banged his gavel.

"Solicitor General," he said. "Please regain your composure so that you may air your grievances like a gentleman."

"Grievances? This is a treasonous outrage!" Wedderburn shouted. "Franklin is a scourge on the back of Mother England!"

The printing presses at London's *Public Adviser* were hot that day. The master typecaster had not seen such incendiary content sitting upon his desk for publication since the letters of Junius—but the author of this letter did not hide behind a pseudonym. This was Dr. Benjamin Franklin, the revered polymath-statesman, claiming responsibility for leaking the Hutchinson Letters to the American press for publication. They were burning Hutchinson and Oliver in effigy on Boston Common, for chritsake! With shaky hands, the master typecaster arranged his fonts on the typeform and pulled down hard on the lever, stamping a test press. The headline read,

INVENTOR AND STATESMAN Dr. BENJAMIN FRANK-LIN INCITES RIOTS IN THE AMERICAN COLONIES AGAINST THE CROWN OF MOTHER ENGLAND!

Of course, the gossip was rampant in the King's Arms Tavern. Two House Of Commons Lords in velvet smocks and curly white wigs sat with their pewter tankards of porter, talking politics with an air of great importance.

"I fear the political influence of Dr. Franklin on this country is far too great," said one of the Lords.

"The man has captured the hearts and minds of the entire House Of Commons," said the other Lord.

"Franklin is a spy," said the first. "I trust the rapscallion about as far as I can throw him."

A pewter tankard slammed down on their table, spilling forth a thick head of porter. The men looked up to find their subject of conversation standing over them.

"Good day, gentleman," Franklin said. "Mind if I join you?"

Franklin took a seat at their bench, without a response from the stunned Lords.

"I could not help but overhear your conversation," he continued. "Perhaps I can shed some light on the matter."

The Lords were red-faced, having been caught in their gossip about the famous statesman now in their midst. Franklin relished the opportunity to further their embarrassment.

"You see, I am a Colonist but first, I am a Briton. My affection and loyalty to Mother England runs through me like the blood in my veins. However, the Colonists will not stand to be unfairly taxed so that the King's coffers can grow fatter while they starve…and I will not stand by and allow it to happen."

Franklin stood, retrieved his porter, chugged the entire thing, and slammed the empty pewter tankard back down on the table.

"Powder your wigs with that one, boys," he said. "Good day."

Back at 36 Craven Street, Elizabeth's condition was deteriorating. Hewson and Polly knelt at her bedside while Mima fed her the occasional spoonful of soup. She was pale and weak. Her symptoms reminded Hewson of Gordon, his recent surgery patient. His intuition screamed. He placed his hand on her neck and felt around.

"I think she has a growth," he said.

"A growth?" said Polly. Was her husband actually delusional like Franklin said, or could this be a real diagnosis?

"Yes," said Hewson. "I recently came across one in surgery. They are quite harmful–deadly even–but they can be removed."

Polly was horrified but hopeful. "What should we do?" she asked.

Hewson felt around Dorothy's again. "I am going to remove it," he said.

He picked up his child and walked her to the dining room table, where he set her down. Then, he rolled his cloth of scalpals out on the table top. Hewson had an apothecary flask or two of laudanum in his private stash–it was a rare and precious anesteshia he reserved only for the gravest emergency. He could think of no better use for it than to make his daughter's surgery more comfortable while he did what he could to save her life. It was at this moment Hewson flashed back to that defining moment when he buried his twin sister and resolved to learn the study of the blood so that no one should have to suffer as she did. Images passed before his mind's eye as vividly as though he were actually back in England's grey north. He saw a freshly dug grave at the bottom of which sat a small coffin made for a child with a little cross carved into the top. He saw a handful of dirt splatter across the wood, some falling inside of the wooden cross. He heard the Vicar drone on in his dreadful sanctimonious way,

"All go to the same place," Hewson heard him say.

Hewson shook himself from this daydream, then took a deep breath and stroked his daughter's head.

"You are going to be all right, my love," he assured her.

The surgeon went down to the cellar to grab the flask of laudanum. When he entered the cellar, he found Franklin standing over a body on the operating table. Upon closer inspection, Hewson could see the body was that of a child–a little boy, no more than five years old. King was also there, assisting in the surgery. Franklin had his forefinger and thumb inside of a hole in the boy's forehead. He extracted the pinael gland, dropped it into a mason jar filled with clear liquid, and screwed the lid on tight.

What he saw, coupled with the stress of his own child lying on the operating table upstairs, almost broke Hewson. Then, a moment of grace—his survival instincts flooded in, turning his horror into rage.

"Is this a souse scrapped off the streets of Gin Lane?" he said through gritted teeth.

"Relax, Job. The kid was born drunk," Franklin replied. "This is the only useful thing he will ever do." Franklin placed the jar containing the fresh pineal gland on the shelf beside the others.

Hewson's rage seized him completely and without thinking, he ran to the shelf where sat the jars of pineal glands. He grabbed Franklin's most recent acquisition and held it over his head, ready to smash.

"Go ahead," Franklin said, stoic and unmoving. "Destroy them all. It will only prompt me to go out and get more. It is the thrill of the chase for me—I revel in this work."

Realizing the futility of his actions, Hewson set the jar on the shelf, grabbed his flask of laudanum, and headed up the steps.

Franklin shouted up after him, "Remember your vows, brother Job!"

Hewson did not look back. In a hurry, he rushed to his daughter's side. Polly was alarmed at the sudden change in her husband's behavior. He was wild-eyed and manic.

"What is it?" she asked.

"We must leave now," said Hewson. "There is no time to pack a bag, we must go now."

"What?" asked Polly, incredulous. She looked to her daughter on the table—Elizabeth was too weak to even keep her eyes open. She looked to Mima, who stood there stunned, awaiting the next development. Confusion–utter confusion–clouded the anxious moment. Her face felt hot, as though she might pass out or vomit.

"What are you talking about?" she managed.

Hewson's eyes grew even wider still, hot with mania.

"Franklin is a murderer–he's in the basement right now with the body of a child," he said as he grabbed his wife by the arm. She pulled away.

"You are mad!" she shouted.

"I am not mad," he said containing his anger, knowing this moment required action, not emotion. He had to get his family out now.

King burst into the dining room, followed closely by Franklin. The slave wrestled the thin surgeon to the ground, easily overpowering him though he flailed about wildly. Polly watched in horror as King tied her husband's hands behind his back and carried him away, kicking and screaming.

"I am not mad!" he shouted.

Down in the cellar, King tied Hewson to a chair in front of the operating table. Hewson was grateful they had already put the body of the child in the stone box–he couldn't bare to see that image again.

Franklin watched as King secured the rope around Hewson's body and the chair. "What are you going to do to me?" Hewson asked.

"We are not going to do anything to you, my boy," he said. "You are simply going to go away for a little while to get the help you need."

Hewson's vengeful eyes stared into the bottomless pit of Franklin's.

Outside of 36 Craven Street, the coachman whipped his horses into motion. Exhausted and helpless, with hands tied behind his back, Hewson stared out the window of the coach at Polly standing on the front doorstep beside Franklin and King. He had lost,

Franklin had won. The old bastard had his family in the palm of his hand, thought Hewson. In fact, Polly belonged to Franklin first. The man had raised her from childhood—there was no world in which she would question his motives, even for a minute. Rationality returned once Hewson's temper settled a bit and he resolved to not let it get the best of him again. At this point, his life depended on how well he played the game in which he was now trapped. There was a way out—he just had to find it. Then he would select the right moment to take Franklin down—he made a private vow to be ready when the opportunity presented itself.

After a several hours-long and cold ride through the English countryside, he saw it in the distance, rising out of the mist like a stone galleon ship sailing to hell–The Bethlem Royal Hospital. The coach pulled into a roundabout in front of the entrance to this palace of misery, where stood two large men in black frocks, waiting. Hewson watched as they approached the coach, coming for him. One of the men opened the door while the other grabbed Hewson by the chain of his handcuffs and pulled him out. He grabbed Hewson from under the arms and the other man grabbed his feet and together they carried him up the steps to the forboding building. As the men carried Hewson inside he saw a Roman marble bas relief over the entrance of two muscular bald men in chains with scrolls under each. One read "melancholy," and the other, "raving."

Once inside, the men shoved Hewson into an open room filled with neglected lunatics, men and women alike. The place stunk to high heaven—a real picture of hell. The only light in the dank room shone through a single square window smaller than a person's head and secured with wooden bars. Hewson took in his new surroundings. Many of the men were bald and half-naked, some totally nude. A nicely dressed aristocrat woman wearing a bonnet and dress fanned her face while talking to herself. A large, naked bald man sat on the ground scratching his face and moaning. A brave nurse tried to keep the man from scratching but he struck her with the back of his hand and proceeded to scratch his face bloody. Another bald man wearing a frock and nickers sat by himself, dejected, staring off into space. There was a musician wearing a cape over his head, playing a scratchy violin while a fairy man danced around like the mythical creature Pan, pretending to play the flute. Hewson's hands were still tied behind his back. He slumped against a wall and sank to the ground. This was his home for the foreseeable future. After what seemed an eternity, he drifted off to sleep. Suddenly, he awoke.

"Hello, Job," a voice said.

A fat doctor wearing a monocle and an "all-seeing eye" necklace stood over Hewson. It took a moment, but soon he recognized this man from his last masonic initiation when he was forced to sodomize another man while wearing a goat's head. A shudder of pain surged through him like a thunderbolt.

"Don't worry, son," said the fat doctor. "I am an old friend of Dr. Franklin. Sometimes all we need to get well is a little rest. I will be monitoring your progress here."

The fat doctor led Hewson down a long hallway. They passed several open rooms where spectators watched chained lunatics receiving bizzare and cruel treatments at the hands of their captors. The nurses administering the treatments were musular, brutish men capable of manhandling any patient. The fat doctor led Hewson slowly, so that could take in the sights.

"I understand you are suffering from a bout of acute mania," said the fat doctor.

They stopped in front of a room where a group of London tourists watched a nurse flogging a chained woman with a large fish, her face sliced bloody from the fins of the fish. They continued on. In another room, more tourists watched a naked man chained to the wall, writhing and covered in leeches. Next, the fat doctor brought Hewson to a room where a patient, seated in a swivel chair suspended upside down from the ceiling, was being spun around in fast circles by one of the brutish nurses. When the chair finally slowed to a stop, the patient vomited into a pile on the floor. The nurse then resumed the spinning.

"We shall begin your treatment by purging your ailments with rotating therapy," said the fat doctor.

The fat doctor led Hewson to the next room where a nurse was performing a lobotomy using a foot-long needle through the nose of a screaming patient.

"If rotating therapy fails," the fat doctor continued, "we will try this."

A nurse opened a large metal door to a dark cell from which ambient moaning emanated. Another nurse shoved Hewson inside and closed the metal door. From inside the darkness, Hewson saw a small slot of the door open and the fat doctor's eyes peering in.

"First, you must rest here a while," he said. "I will be back in several days to check on your progress." The last bit of light was shut out with the closing of the slot, and Hewson found himself in total darkness, so that he could not see his own hand held right in front of his face, even after his eyes had time to adjust. He was alone with the moans of his prisoner companions and the stench of their unwashed bodies, urine, and feces.

CHAPTER 18

WELL AGAIN

JOSEPH DUPLESSIS' FINISHED iconic portrait of Benjamin Franklin hung above the fireplace mantel in an ornate gold frame. A month had passed since Hewson was sent to the Bethlem Royal Hospital. Now he was back at 36 Craven Street. Franklin was sitting in his chair reading a book when King entered, followed by Hewson, his eyes vacant, his gait stiff and strange.

"William, my boy. Are you feeling well-rested?" Franklin asked, not looking up from his book.

"Yes. Very much so," Hewson spoke in monotone.

"Good," said Franklin. He knew they had taken good care of him.

Elizabeth lay in bed—her condition had further deteriorated in her father's absence. She was pale and so weak she could hardly keep her eyes open. Polly and Hewson stood at her bedside, but her father might as well have not even been in the room. His eyes were vacant and hollow. Polly was worn from grief, her eyes puffy and red. She wondered at her husband. What had happened to him at Bethlem Royal? As far as his actions showed, the sick girl lying there could have been an inadequate object–a piece of furniture. She fought back the tears as she had done for the last month or more.

"Our daughter is not doing well, William," she said. "I fear this may be the end." With that, she broke down sobbing. Hewson simply stood there, staring off into space.

"Oh god, I wish you were here" she moaned. She grabbed her husband's face and kissed him, tears falling freely from her eyes. She kissed his lips, his cheek, his forehead. Hewson was nonreactive–he stood there motionless, like a mannequin, eyes wide and staring.

That night at dinner, the order of events played out as if nothing had changed. But everything had changed. Hewson was different now. Knives sliced into pheasants on silver platters. Franklin ate his plate full of veggies. King stood by, keeping the wine flowing for the Widow Mrs. Stevenson, who was drunk as usual. The Widow downed another glass and King refilled it. Hewson stared off into space, blank, emotionless. Occasionally, he took a slow bite of food and chewed it with his mouth open. Little pieces of half-chewed food dropped out of his mouth and back onto the plate. Polly couldn't even look at him. Her eyes filled with tears. The dinner was a tense, silent affair.

Afterward, Hewson sat alone by the fire, staring into the flames. Polly sat at the dining room table sobbing while Mima cleared the dishes. Franklin slid in beside her, rubbing her back, consoling her.

"Will he ever be right again?" she asked.

"Only time will tell, my dear," said Franklin. "Only time will tell. Until then, all we can do is be here to support his recovery."

When Franklin felt his soothing words had sufficiently comforted the grieving Polly, he next went to the smoking room. Using his cane to balance, he eased himself down into the tall velvet chair across from Hewson, beside the fire.

"Ah," Franklin groaned, having just eased himself into the chair. "'Tis' not an easy thing, growing old. Is it?"

Hewson remained silent, staring into the fire.

"I understand it may be too soon yet, but when you have it in you" continued Franklin, "I would like you to assist in my next surgery."

Like some kind of horrible reptile, Hewson turned his head toward Franklin and nodded "yes."

"Very good," said Franklin, much pleased. They had taken *very* good care of Hewson at Bethlam Royal. Very good, indeed.

In the middle of the night, Hewson opened his eyes wide. He peeled back the sheet and slipped out of bed, careful not to wake his sleeping wife. He crept into the children's room and over to his daughter's bed, being careful not to wake her twin brother, who was lying asleep in his bed at the other side of the room. Elizabeth's eyes opened when Hewson peeled back her bedsheets and she made a gasp but she was too weak to make a sound loud enough to wake her sleeping brother. Hewson picked her up out of bed and crept back out of the room with her, quiet as a mouse.

Down in the cellar, Elizabeth lay on the operating table with two oil lamps burning beside her head for light. Hewson selected his last flask of laudanum from the shelf beside the pineal jars. He uncorked the flask and poured the contents into Elizabeth's weak mouth and she closed her eyes.

Then, a vision from the past flashed before Hewson's eyes. He stood over the grave of his twin sister holding a handful of dirt. He heard the tiresome Vicar drone, "All come from dust and to dust all return," and he threw his handful of dirt into the grave.

Hewson took a deep breath. All the events of his life had led him to this moment. If he was to be remembered for anything at all, let it be saving his daughter's life. His eyes hardend, determind to succeed. He unrolled his cloth of scalpals out on the table with a new resolve.

"You are going to be all right my love," he said, stroking his daughter's hair. Then, he took another deep breath and steadied himself for his most difficult surgery yet. He picked up a scalpal and set to work.

Polly rolled over in her sleep and feeling the empty space in the bed beside her, awakened with a gasp. Realizing her husband was indeed missing from the bed, she sat up and scrambled in the darkness to lit the oil lamp at her bedside. Holding the lamp, she made her way down the hall and into the children's room. She peered inside, and to her horror, saw Elizabeth's empty bed. She let out a scream and took of running down the hall, down the stairs, and into the dining room, waking every body in the house. Franklin and King found her standing over the dining room table, over the body of her daughter, her mouth agape in shock. Elizabeth lay unconscious on the dining room table, a bloody cloth tourniquet tied around her neck. Where was her husband?

Hewson was long gone, walking London's late night stones toward Gin Lane, where the skeletal drunks were out in full force, crawling and writhing like monstrous earthworms. Dr. Hunter was the only one who could help him now–he had to find his old mentor. Hewson came upon the old Anatomical Theatre where he started this mad journey one thousand years ago. He stopped dead in his tracks–the great stone building had been gutted by fire, the outsisde scarred black with soot from the flames. He rushed to the door and tried to open it but the door was locked. What had happened here? His eyes searched the outside of the building for any other possible way in, when a black hand wearing an emerald ring crossed over his mouth from behind and grabbed his face. The dark figure wrestled Hewson to the stones, knocking him unconscious. On the ground, the angel of death straddled Hewson's body, removed the emerald ring, flipped open the stone and poured its deadly contents into his mouth. Arsenic. King's stoic face showed no sign of remorse. He knew this fate was better for Hewson than what Franklin and the masons had in mind. He stood and walked away, leaving the surgeon's body in the street for dead.

Dr. Hunter walked the early morning streets with his current protege, a young man with the hair of an old-fashioned pageboy. He pushed a cadaver in a wooden cart, following Dr. Hunter to his lab. Although four years prior an angry mob had gutted the lab by fire, Hunter secured a grant to have the interior rebuilt and was again using the building for his lectures. As they came upon Gin Lane, the old anatomist spotted a well-dressed man lying face down in the street. He approached the sleeping gentleman and had his protege turn him over. It was a shocking sight.

"My god, William?" the words lept from Dr. Hunter's mouth without his permission. He bent down and slapped Hewson's face to wake him. His old protégé came to little by little, his eyes rolling around in his head, slack-jawed and drooling, mumbling nonsense to himself.

"Come on chap, let's get you some help," said the good mentor.

Dr. Hunter's pageboy protégé slung Hewson onto the cart atop the cadaver, and they made haste to return the drunken blood surgeon back to his home at 36 Craven Street. King helped Dr. Hunter's protégé inside with Hewson's confused and barely conscious body. They brought him upstairs and laid him in his bed to sleep it off. Polly could not believe her eyes. Her husband was never much of a drinker. In fact, she had never seen him more than a little merry off of Christmas wine. Seeing her husband a blubbering puddle of his former self was more alarming than seeing him lobotomized.

Hunter and Franklin stood at the doorway, talking. "He was lying in the street, very drunk," Dr. Hunter explained.

"I am not surprised," Dr. Franklin replied. "The poor boy has been having grave problems. He recently left Bedlam after a month's rest."

"I see," Hunter said.

"Thank God you found him," said Franklin.

"Indeed. I am glad he is back in good hands. See to it the boy gets well, Dr. Franklin. He is at the top of his field."

There was a longing in Hunter's voice. Franklin relished in knowing that if he couldn't have Hewson, nobody would. There was no risk of losing him now—he was already gone.

"Of course," said Dr. Franklin. "We will take good care of him."

That night, the fat doctor from Bethlem Royal Hospital appeared. He sat on the edge of Hewson's bed, holding his tongue down with a metal tool and checking inside of his mouth. Life was draining from Hewson's sweaty green face.

"Say AHH for me," said the fat doctor.

Hewson let out a soft moan. Polly stood in the corner, her hands to her face. She had been with him all day, beside herself with worry and grief. She began to weep.

"Doctor, this is more than simply drink," she said.

"He may have contracted sepsis from working with an infected cadaver," said the monocled doctor through his pudgy, distorted mouth.

Something about him pierced Polly's stomach with a shudder of revulsion. Her nausea grew as he leaned in closer.

"This might also account for his mounting insanity," said the doctor. "I propose a bloodletting."

In his final moment, Hewson saw the golden amulet of the all seeing eye shining from around the fat doctor's neck. Finally, freedom from this madness. He surged toward the light.

Polly and the fat doctor looked to Hewson. He had ceased breathing, his eyes locked in a stare to the ceiling. Polly let out a wail, and Franklin appeared, receiving her into his arms. Over Polly's sobbing shoulder, Franklin motioned toward Hewson with his head. The fat doctor picked up on this cue. He removed the "all-seeing-eye" amulet from around Hewson's neck and handed it to Franklin while Polly sobbed in his arms.

CHAPTER 19

JUDAS IN EXILE

IN A DARK room, two cloaked and hooded men stood before a skyline of dripping wax candles.

"Judas," one of the cloaked men said.

Franklin was sitting in the dark room among the other members, all surrounded by candles. He stood.

"What is under the flowerbed?" the other cloaked figure asked.

"My protege and I are conducting anatomical experiments," said Franklin.

"With drunkards?" one of the cloaked men asked.

"We saw you and Job escort a rather bosky fellow down there under the cover of night," said the other.

Franklin stood stoic, motionless.

"Surely this was not one of your charitable works?" the cloaked figure continued.

"Perhaps you will bring us to see your findings?" said the other. "After all, there are no secrets between us."

Down in the cellar at 36 Craven Street, Franklin watched as the cloaked and hooded men rummaged through his journals and the pineal gland jars on the shelves of his makeshift laboratory. The cloaked men held large sacks, which they filled with Franklin's journals and the jars. Lord North bagged up the pineal gland jars and David Hume collected the journals. Hume opened one of the journals to a page with a heading that read:

A COMPLETE MAP OF THE HUMAN SOUL

Below this was a perfectly hand-drawn Sri Yantra mandala surrounded by strange mathematical equations. Hume flipped through the journal, which was filled with diagrams of the pineal glands and sacred geometry supported by more strange mathematical equations and pages of writing.

"Rest assured, Judas," Hume said. "Your memory will live on forever in the souls of men but not for this. This one is *ours*."

Franklin struggled against his rage—there was nothing he could do.

"Your amulet," said Lord North.

Franklin removed the "all-seeing-eye" from around his neck and placed it in Lord North's open hand.

The Privy Council had assembled in the Cockpit at Whitehall for the trial of Dr. Benjamin Franklin regarding the leaking of the Hutchinson Letters. Lord North presided over the trial which was presently chugging along. Solicitor General Lord Wedderburn—the prosecuting attorney—withhis long white hair hanging roundly past his shoulders like two giant teardrops, looked like the human version of an Afghan hound or an Irish setter. Wearing his signature long-flowing bright red velvet robe, he stood among the other members of the Privy Council. Franklin stood before them, alone in the Cockpit.

In a room jammed to capacity with Lords of the Council, politicians, and spectators, including the Lunaticks of the Lunar Society,

Solicitor General Wedderburn led a brutal attack on Franklin's character for the leaking of the Hutchinson Letters.

Franklin stood before the council like a rock, his head resting on his left hand propped up on his right arm crossed over his chest, not moving, enduring the pitiless storm.

"Dr. Benjamin Franklin admitted to deliberately leaking private letters, regarding Offical Matters of the Crown, to the Boston Press for publication in order to incite a Colonial Revolution," Wedderburn shouted, hot in the face, "This is an act of treason!"

The crowd erupted but Franklin was unmoved. Lord North banged his gavel but the crowd kept cheering. The Lunaticks watched as their brother Masons fulfilled their Destiny. Lord North banged his gavel over and over again, until finally, the crowd settled down.

"Thank you, Solicitor General," said Lord North. "You may be seated."

Wedderburn took his seat with contempt. He was not a Mason, and took this business of exiling Franklin very seriously, as if none of it was planned by his own superiors. The Solicitor General was oblivious—he thought he actually functioned with some degree of autonomy in this stately drama. I'm his mind, he was responsible for upholding the ideals of his Country.

"Benjamin Franklin," said Lord North. "After decades of Faithful service to the Crown as Postmaster General and Ambassador of the Colonies, the Privy Council hereby relieves you of your duties. No further services will be required."

Franklin stood stoic, unmoved.

The following week, Franklin stood on the deck of a great big clipper ship with Polly, her twin children, and the good slave King at his side, looking into the wind as they sailed the high seas toward America.

The End.